D1360646

SUNSET WINS

Center Point
Large Print

Also by Max Brand® and available from
Center Point Large Print:

The Cure of Silver Cañon
The Red Well
Lightning of Gold
Daring Duval
Sour Creek Valley
Gunfighters in Hell
Red Hawk's Trail
Sun and Sand

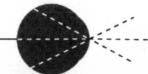

SUNSET
WINS

A Western Trio

Max Brand®

CENTER POINT LARGE PRINT
THORNDIKE, MAINE

This Circle Ⓥ Western is published by
Center Point Large Print in the year 2018 in
co-operation with Golden West Literary Agency.

Copyright © 2018 by Golden West Literary Agency.

All rights reserved.

First Edition
November, 2018

The name Max Brand® is a registered trademark
with the United States Patent and Trademark Office
and cannot be used for any purpose
without express written permission.

Printed in the United States of America
on permanent paper.
Set in 16-point Times New Roman type.

ISBN: 978-1-68324-997-9

Library of Congress Cataloging-in-Publication Data

Names: Brand, Max, 1892-1944, author.
Title: Sunset wins : a western trio / Max Brand.
Description: First edition. | Thorndike, Maine :
    Center Point Large Print, 2018. | Series: A Circle V western
Identifiers: LCCN 2018033715 | ISBN 9781683249979
    (hardcover : alk. paper)
Subjects: LCSH: Large type books. | Western stories.
Classification: LCC PS3511.A87 A6 2018b | DDC 813/.54—dc23
LC record available at https://lccn.loc.gov/2018033715

SUNSET WINS

ACKNOWLEDGMENTS

"The Gift" by Max Brand was first published in *Western Story Magazine* (12/24/21). Copyright © 1921 by Street & Smith Publications, Inc. Copyright © renewed 1949 by Dorothy Faust. Acknowledgment is made to Condé Nast Publications, Inc., for their co-operation.

"Jerico's Garrison Finish" by John Frederick in *Western Story Magazine* (5/21/21). Copyright © 1921 by Street & Smith Publications, Inc. Copyright © renewed 1949 by Dorothy Faust. Acknowledgment is made to Condé Nast Publications, Inc., for their co-operation.

" 'Sunset' Wins" by George Owen Baxter in *Western Story Magazine* (4/7/23). Copyright © 1923 by Street & Smith Publications, Inc. Copyright © renewed 1951 by Dorothy Faust. Acknowledgment is made to Condé Nast Publications, Inc., for their co-operation.

THE GIFT

I

There was not a breath of wind. The storm which had howled across the mountains for well-nigh a fortnight was now gone. It left the summits and all the higher valleys moon-white with snow. And over this snow the moon itself, rising early, cast the dark pointed shadows of the pines. The silence was as profound as the arch of the sky, as pure as the shining stars. It was a hallowed quiet, well fitted for this night above all nights, Christmas Eve.

Over the white summit the rider came like a stain, and the shape of his galloping horse, struggling, misshapen over crusted snows beside him, made a bitter contrast with the still shadows of the pines. The rider brought an element of labor and effort into a place where there should have been only the white, sleeping mountains and the dark, sleeping trees.

But he saw no beauty in what lay around him, and because he saw no beauty, all beauty ceased to exist. The peaks and their forested sides became of less importance. The whole focus of interest was on that lonely, frightened horseman.

About his fear there was no doubt. When he reached a hilltop, he invariably looked back and sighed with relief when he saw, perhaps, an empty upslope behind. Yet his sense of security was ever short-lived, and the next instant he would be spurring wildly down the grade beyond, as though danger dogged him in the very shadow of his horse.

He came headlong as a landslide into the great hush of Bender Valley, coursing through the trees almost regardless of the windings of the trail, then sheering straight off to the left, where there was no trail at all, only the solidity of the forest. The panting of his horse, the grunt of pain as the poor beast slipped and recovered in the snow, became more audible in the quiet of this wood. Trees are almost like mirrors. They reflect the souls of those who come among them. To Shorty Dugan these pines seemed stealing close to him, listening and watching and keeping the tidings of that which they had seen.

Still he spurred. And under the goad the pinto lunged ahead with shrinking quarters, as though into a collar, without really increasing his speed. That collar was utter exhaustion. He went no faster, because it was impossible for the outworn mustang to swing his legs faster or drive them more strongly through the snow.

He stumbled into a little clearing. It was so small that the trees seemed to lean out toward it from all sides. Shorty Dugan flung himself out of the saddle and landed in the snow, sprawling and slipping, for long riding had numbed his legs.

The horse, relieved from the burden, dropped his head, spread his trembling legs, and puffed great clouds of frosty breath into the moonshine. Shorty flung the beast a curse over his shoulder as he regained his footing; it was Shorty's habit to curse the nearest living object whenever a mishap overtook him.

Then he stumbled on toward the cabin. It was very small. The shadow from the eastern tree-tops cut across it. One half of the cabin was lost in blackness. The other half was dead-white in the moonshine and, against this whiteness like a jewel on a dead face, a yellow lamplight glimmered in a single window.

In spite of his haste, Shorty checked his rush. He stole to the side of the shack, peered through under a shading hand at the interior of the lighted room, and then, nodding in satisfaction, hurried back toward the front door. No sooner had he opened it and sprung into the darkness within—for his agility redoubled as the blood ran warm again through his muscles—than the door was slammed shut again and he himself was tripped and pitched to his face, falling right into the yellow shaft of light that came through the open door of the room in which he had seen the lamp.

He yelled as he dropped, whirled in falling, and tugged at his gun, but he found himself lying on his back, looking up along the barrel of a long

Colt and into a quiet, thin, shadowy face behind it.

"Don't!" he gasped. "Don't! I'm Shorty! Don't shoot!"

The other touched him scornfully with a toe and slipped his gun back into its holster.

"Get up!" he commanded.

Shorty obediently clambered back to his feet.

"Don't you know me?" he kept whimpering. "Don't you know I'm all right? Don't you know me?"

"I don't know nobody," said the man of the cabin. "I don't know nobody that comes tearing into my house without knocking or nothing."

"I seen you sitting all quiet in your chair in the other room a minute ago and I thought . . . and . . . I'm Shorty. You know me?"

This disjointed and frightened speech made the tall man smile.

"I don't know you," he said in a grave tone, which had in it a certain hardness of contempt. "I ain't seen you for three months. Maybe you ain't what you used to be."

"Wait till you hear what I got to tell you!" exclaimed Shorty. "Maybe you think I been bought off or something. Is that it?"

"Go inside where I can get a look at you," ordered the host.

Shorty obeyed, and he was followed into the cozy little living room by the other. They were

14

opposed types. Shorty lived up to his name. He had the short, bowed legs which generally connote strength. A barrel chest, short, thick neck, bulldog face, and fighting features made him, so far as was physically possible, different from the lithe man of the cabin. The other was above six feet in height and looked still taller. He had gray eyes, almost colorless and very steady, and his thin features were of a cruelly predatory cast. His contempt and reserve now had a biting edge.

"In the old days," he said, "as chief I would've horsewhipped a gent that come blundering in like this." He added, as though aware that he had gone too far: "Not that that's really my way. Only, I don't like to be busted in on like this. Lucky for you I waited to make out who you were."

Shorty changed color. "You might of knowed by the way I come smashing in that I was a friend."

"Never mind what I knowed. You said you had a message for me?"

"A big one, too," said Shorty, swelling suddenly with importance. "Happy Jack's coming! Happy Jack himself!"

"Never heard of him. Who's he?"

"Who's he?" gasped Shorty. "You don't know Happy? Why . . . why . . ."

He blundered hopelessly, as a man will when confronted with the necessity of defining some great abstraction. Suppose one were to be asked to define lightning.

"You remember young Jackson," began Shorty, feeling his way toward an explanation, "the gent you had us bunco out of the claim? The gent that Murphy drilled?"

"Well?"

"Happy Jack's his friend. He found out that you were behind the killing, and he's started on your trail."

"And you come a hundred and fifty . . . two hundred miles to tell me that? To tell me that some gent I never heard of is out for me? Say, Shorty, are you plumb crazy? Do you know me?"

This biting contempt stung Shorty. The blood gathered dark in his tanned face.

"Listen, chief," he said, "you know these parts, but you don't know things in the south. Was Murphy a good man with a gun?"

"Was he a good man?" answered the other, frowning. "Yes, and he still is. One of the very best. I trained him myself. How come you say 'was'?"

"He'll never pull a gat again," answered Shorty, reveling in this chance of overwhelming the other. "He'll never pull a gun again, Sandy Crisp."

With a profound relish he watched the gray eyes of Crisp contract and glitter beneath the colorless, bushy brows.

"Happy Jack met him. There was a fair gun

16

play. Jack beat him a mile. Jack shot him down. He smashed Murphy's shoulder to smithereens. Murphy'll never pull a gun again."

Sandy moistened his colorless lips. "Go on," he said almost gently.

"He found out from Murphy, Happy did," went on Shorty, "that you was behind the buncoing and the killing of young Jackson, the tenderfoot. Seems Jackson used to be a friend of his. Happy was on the trail of them that done for him. When he found out that Murphy was only a tool of yours, he left Murphy and started north. Then I come like a whirlwind. I've changed horses twice, and the plug I got outside is plumb spent. Chief, climb on your horse and run."

There was more curiosity than fear in the manner of the chief.

"You think I'd better not wait for him? Not even with you here to help me? Or will he come with a band?"

"He's a lone rider, chief. But you ain't going to have me here with you. No, sir! I'm gone again, *pronto*. I know how good you are. I've seen you work half a dozen times. I ain't any slouch myself when it comes to a pinch. But stay here and wait for Happy?" He laughed without mirth in his voice. "Nope, I ain't tired of life."

"He's as bad an actor as all that, eh?"

"Go south," said Shorty. "Go south and ask about him."

17

"What's he done?"

"Plenty. And he's so good that he don't have to shoot to kill. He fights for the love of fighting. That's all. And he's so fast and so sure with a gat that he just nicks a gent and drops him."

"I've heard about that kind." The chief curled his lip as he spoke.

"I've seen him do it," said Shorty, with an ire of almost religious awe. "I've seen him do it." His voice was hardly more than a whisper. "He could've killed Murphy ten times. He didn't."

"You saw the fight and didn't try to help Murphy?"

"I saw the fight and buckled the flap of my holster, so that devil wouldn't pay no attention to me."

"Hmm," muttered the other. "This gent hypnotizes folks, maybe. Old?"

"Young."

"How's he look?"

"Fine looking. Clean as a whistle. Blue eyes. Tall as you and big, heavy shoulders and a tapering build."

"And you think I wouldn't have no chance against him?"

"I don't think. I know."

"I've never been beat, Shorty."

"I know. But this gent . . . I don't know how it is . . . but I figure his luck is all before him. He ain't used it up yet. The time ain't come for him to lose. So long, chief. I'm gone."

"Wait a minute, you fool! Does he know . . . did Murphy tell him . . . where this cabin is?"

"No."

"Then he'll never get me. Nobody knows about it except our boys."

"He'll find it. He'll smell it out."

"How?"

"How does a buzzard find a dead one when it's clean out of sight?" asked Shorty.

He waited for no more talk, but flung himself out of the room, and Sandy Crisp went to the window and pressed his face close to the frosted glass after rubbing out an eyehole. He saw Shorty mount with frantic haste and, glancing over his shoulder, spur his reeling cow pony into the shadow of the trees. There was something ludicrous in his fear of nothingness, and it set Sandy smiling.

· The smile was still lingering on his lips when he turned from the window and saw, leaning against the doorjamb, a tall, broad-shouldered youth who was rolling a cigarette. But his blue eyes were not fastened on his work, they were regarding, with a sort of amusement, the features of his host.

II

Whatever the thoughts which passed through the agile mind of Sandy Crisp—and judging by the flicker of his glance about the room there were many—the idea of striking at once at the invader was not executed. Instead, he deliberately turned his back on the silent visitor, walked across the room, drew up a chair before the fire on the open hearth, and waved the stranger to another seat.

"Sit down and rest your legs, Happy," he said. "Sit down and make yourself to home. If you're cold inside as well as out, I got some moonshine that ain't half bad."

"Thanks," said the other, lighting his cigarette with a deft left hand, as Sandy noted with a side glance. "I see that kind these days when liquor's hard to come at, but I don't use the stuff myself. It's hard on the eyes."

Sandy Crisp nodded, grinning.

"I didn't think you'd come in on that old game," he said, "but a gent never can tell. Sometimes the wisest step into the oldest door. Sit down?"

"Sure."

Happy Jack walked slowly across the room. The moment he came into the yellow of the firelight, Sandy could appreciate how truly big and powerful the stranger was, and the easy grace which told of strong muscles flowing in smooth harmony. He was handsome in a singularly boyish way. His face was brown as a berry, which made his eyes a more startling blue. His whole expression gave an index to mischief, rather than cruelty, in the heart of the man. A single glance at his face was enough to justify his nickname: Happy. In age he might be from twenty-four to twenty-six. This faint, quizzical smile with which he now regarded his host made him seem even younger. Sandy was favoring him with an equally calm regard.

"You don't seem in no special hurry," remarked Happy Jack.

"I'm not," answered Sandy. "I'm trying to place you. I seen you somewhere once."

"Ever been south as far as Tuckertown?"

"Nope."

"Then you've never seen me."

Sandy shook his head. "I've seen you or a ringer for you," he went on genially. "Well, kid, you've sure got ambitious, ain't you? Stepping right out to make a name for yourself by dropping Sandy Crisp."

His cold mockery did not disturb the quiet content that brooded ceaselessly in the blue eyes of the stranger. His expression was as mild as that of a child when it sees a new and curious toy for the first time.

"I ain't been thinking about collecting any fame

21

for myself," he answered, smiling and showing a flashing line of white teeth. "You see, down my way they don't know you, Crisp. You ain't even a name."

"I guess you'll have to tell 'em about me, then," went on Sandy, still sneering to break down the nerve of the younger man.

"I don't advertise much," replied the other.

Sandy Crisp bit his lip. This was not at all to his liking. Such perfect solidity of calm amazed him. His mind reverted to something Shorty had said. The luck of this handsome youth seemed all before him and undrained. Calamity, failure, could not even be dreamed of in connection with those laughing blue eyes. All that could be wondered at was the possibility that fighting rage, the lust for battle, would come into that boyish face. It was inconceivable. A strange hollowness appeared, now, in Sandy Crisp's stomach, a chill struck up along his back. His fingers were growing uncertain. A sense of weakness flowed through him. What could this be?

It was fear! He knew it suddenly and with a devitalizing pang. He, Sandy Crisp, the invincible, the cold-hearted, the dangerous in battle, was afraid. And yet an imp of the perverse drove him on to draw out his young visitor.

"Not fame?" echoed Sandy, sneering now to conceal the whiteness which he felt must be growing about the edges of his mouth. "That ain't what's brought you up here? It was simply because you wanted to get square for the killing of young Jackson, eh? You trying to tell me that you were that fond of the fool?"

"Was he a fool?" answered the other, snapping his cigarette butt into the fire.

As he spoke he lifted his head, and Sandy Crisp saw that the boyishness was gone from the face before him. The nostrils were beginning to quiver, the mouth to straighten.

"He was fool enough to trust men," said Happy Jack. "That's what Jackson was fool enough to do. He trusted me. He put me up and fed me and took care of me and staked me and sent me on my way without ever expecting to get anything back for it. He took me in because I was hungry. And when I went off and got a stake and come back to pay him what I owed him, I found him dead. You hear? Dead!"

He had changed still more while he spoke. He was rising from his chair as though great forces within now fought for a chance to exorcise themselves. And a veritable flame of rage was burning in his eyes.

"Him you call a fool was dead, and you'd done it through your man Murphy. I fixed Murphy, and then I started for you. I've found you, and you're going to pay, Crisp, so that my pal, Jackson, seeing you go down, will know I ain't forgotten what a gent owes to his partner."

He sprang to the center of the room.

"I've come here and waited, hoping to hear you say you were sorry for the dirty murder you had Murphy work. But you ain't sorry for nothing. You killed Jackson. You left his wife and his three kids with nothing to keep them except sorrowing for him you killed. Does that worry you? Not a bit! You got no heart, Crisp, and I'm going to kill you with a smile . . . same's I'd kill a snake or a mad dog, because you ain't a human."

The tirade burst out with incredible emphasis, the words driven through drawn lips. And the whole of Happy Jack's big body trembled from head to foot with his passion. He had been a handsome boy a moment before. He was suddenly a madman.

With a great effort Sandy Crisp retained his smile, for he had known men to go blind with rage in the face of that taunting sarcasm.

"You're tolerable sure you'll finish me, eh?"

"Sure of it? Aye. A thousand times sure. I'm waiting, Sandy. I'm waiting for you to start."

Still, making no move to rise from his chair, partly paralyzed by the chill of fear which was now more and more stiffening his limbs, Sandy Crisp looked up at his antagonist, and always his forehead was creased by the puzzled frown that it had worn from time to time since he first saw the big man from the south.

When would that chill of terror depart from

him? When would he be able to rise to his feet?

Suddenly he knew that he was beaten. Another five minutes of delay, and he would be incapable of action. The terrible certainty of Happy Jack, the certainty to which Shorty had paid such a tribute not long before, was unnerving him. If he fought, he must fight now.

"Once more!" shouted Happy Jack. "Will you stand up, or do I have to come for you bare-handed?"

And as he spoke, he laughed suddenly, wildly, as though the thought of that conflict, man to man and hand to hand, was inexpressibly preferable to the sudden fight of guns. But while he laughed, stealing a long stride nearer to Crisp, the latter thrust out his hand.

"Wait! Happy! Wait!" he called. "I been trying to think. Now I got it. I got the name of the gent you're like in the face. Your laugh showed me."

And he himself fell back into his chair and burst into long-drawn, hysterical laughter, until the tears came into his eyes.

The other stood frowning in wonder and glaring down at Crisp, until the outlaw straightened again with a sudden gesture of friendliness, as if inviting Happy Jack to step into a secret.

"Here you come on a killing trail," he said, the laughter not quite gone from his voice, "and here I sit up to this minute just choosing the place where I was to plant a bullet in you. But as a matter of fact, Happy, we ain't going to fight. Not a bit of it."

"What?" exclaimed the younger man.

"Listen," said the other, growing more grave. "Do you know what we're going to do? We're going to be partners, son. We're going to be partners!"

He laughed again, overflowing with joy.

"Me?" Happy Jack sneered. "I'd rather be partners with a coyote. That's what I say."

"Sure you would, if a coyote could make you rich. But it can't, and I can."

"Crisp," said Happy Jack ominously, "I dunno what the play is that you figure on making. But I wouldn't trust you a split part of a second. If you think you're going to talk me off my guard, you're wild in the head. You can lay to that."

"What would you say," broke in Crisp, "to being the heir to a ranch worth about a million, more or less? What would you say to shaking hands with me and coming into an estate like that?"

"What," said Happy Jack solemnly, "would Jackson say if he seen me shake hands with you?"

The other seized upon this thread of argument.

"Why, he'd be happy, because he'd know, then, that you'd be able to take care of his widow and his kids. Wouldn't that make him happy?"

Jack rubbed his bony knuckles across his chin.

"Go on, Crisp," he said coldly, "I'll wait till you get through talking. If I could make sure of taking care of them four lives . . . well, here it's Christmas time, and it's sure the right season for making gifts, eh?"

He smiled sourly, as though he had no real hope that through Sandy Crisp he might attain this charitable power.

"Sure," Sandy Crisp chuckled, still studying with keener and ever keener interest the face of the man from the south. "And what's more, you're going to be a gift yourself . . . and you're going to be a gift this same night. Come to think of it, this is Christmas Eve, ain't it? The time the old women and the young fools get soft-hearted?"

Happy Jack stared closely at him.

"Yes," he said softly, "the time they get that way." And while he spoke his eyes were as cold as steel.

"Listen," ran on Crisp with a growing enthusiasm, "when you threw back your head and laughed a while back, I seen young Johnny Neilan again, standing on top of the logs in the jam and going down the river. A minute later, while he was laughing and waving his hand at the rest of us boys and knowing well enough that he had about thirty seconds to live, the log turned, he went under, and that was the last ever seen of Johnny."

Happy Jack listened quietly, waiting until the other came to the point of all this talk.

"Well," went on Sandy Crisp, "I'll go back a little ways further. Yonder, over in the hills, where the good range country begins on the far side of the valley, lives old John Neilan and Missus John Neilan, his wife. They're the hardest, closest-fisted, meanest pair in the mountains, and they got enough money to choke a herd of elephants. They got no charity locked up inside of 'em. They pay their hired men less, they feed 'em worse, than folks around here that ain't got half so much coin.

"Twelve years ago they were a pile different, but pretty hard even then. They were so hard, in fact, that they made life miserable for their only child, and that was young Johnny Neilan, Junior. Johnny was going on fourteen, a straight-standing, wild-eyed kid. One day he ups and runs off because the old man had been giving him a tongue-lashing for something. He disappears, anyways, and he never was found, and it plumb busted the hearts of the two old folks. If they was hard before, they got like pure flint afterward.

"Well, nobody got trace of Johnny, till one time I come up to a logging camp in Canada, and among the gents I seen a husky youngster about eighteen that looked pretty much like Johnny Neilan. I couldn't be sure, because kids change so darned much between fourteen and twenty that you could hardly tell your own brother if you was away from him five or six years. Anyway, I laid a trap for the kid and made him confess, after a while, that he was Johnny Neilan. That was the morning of a big jam in the log drive. About ten seconds later, after he'd told me who he was, Johnny had run out onto the jam and was working away. All at once the jam busted. The rest of the boys got off safe. But Johnny was stuck out there by himself. He seen they was no chance to get safe to shore. So he just stood up and waved good bye, laughing. And the next minute he went under and never come up . . . just the way I told you a while back. Twenty logs must've smashed him to bits the minute he went under the surface of the water.

"I come back to these parts, and I dropped in on old Neilan and told him what I seen. Can you believe that the old fool just cussed me out and swore it wasn't true? He and his wife had gone on, all those years, wishing to have the boy back, so that he couldn't stop his wishing even when I told him the out-and-out truth. He took it serious enough to go up north, though, and find that logging camp.

"There he found out that none of the boys had knowed Johnny by his right name. And they gave old Neilan a picture of the boy the way he was just before the logs got him. Well,

Happy, you know how pictures are. Johnny had sure changed a pile in the four years. He was man-sized. And that picture showed him with a face all covered with four days' growth of hair. Old Neilan took one long look and then took a great big breath of relief. He'd just nacherally made up his mind that that wasn't Johnny. His boy was still alive and would come riding back home someday, and everything would be hunky-dory on to the end of the story. You know the way old folks get? Plumb stubborn and foolish? That's the way he got. Wouldn't listen to no sense. And him and his wife are still sure that young John Neilan will come back. And they're right! They're going to see him come back!"

He jumped out of his chair, laughing joyously, and pointed at Happy. "You're the man!"

"Me?" gasped Happy.

"You!" shouted the outlaw. "In about ten minutes after you get there the old man will remember what the kid and him had the argument about the time his kid left. It was because young Johnny got the key to his old man's safe . . . the old fool keeps a pile of cash in his house . . . and got to tinkering with the lock. Old Neilan caught him and raised the devil. Well, he'll be so plumb tickled to have you back that he'll make you a present of the key. All you got to do, then, is to sneak down late tonight, grab the boodle, and then come out to me. I'll have horses ready. Man, we'll clean up a good forty thousand if we clean up a cent."

His ecstasy of greed was sharply checked by the shake of Happy's head.

"You think I'm fool enough to try that?"

"Why not? You're sure like Johnny. Maybe not if he was alive and standing beside you now. But he was a big kid, and you're a big man. You got the same color of hair, the same color of eyes, and the same funny way of throwing your head on one side when you laugh. You can step right into his shoes."

"But suppose they get to talking about old times. . . ."

"Mostly you'll be able to say that you've forgotten a good deal inside of twelve years. And you've only got to stall them off for one evening, or maybe two. Then you can grab the money and kiss 'em all good bye. One minute they have a Christmas present, the next minute they have it not."

He fell again into hearty laughter but stopped short at the shudder of Happy Jack.

"Sandy," said Happy Jack, "do you think I'm skunk enough to fool that poor old man and his wife?"

"Poor old nothing," snorted Sandy. "They're the meanest . . ."

"I've done tolerable bad things in my day," said

31

Happy slowly, "but I wouldn't make money that way."

"Then don't keep the money for yourself," said the elastic-minded Crisp. "Don't keep it at all. Just turn over what you get to Jackson's widow. Ain't you been a lot cut up because her and the three kids didn't have nothing to live on? Well, Happy, you take the coin from them two old skinflints and give it to the widow. That'd sure be a good deed, if you want to fall in with the Christmas idea. Does it sound good to you?"

Happy Jack sighed. For that single instant he was off his guard, staring through the window. Sandy's hand made a furtive motion toward the butt of his gun, but it came away again at once. There was too rich a game in sight to imperil such chances in order to make a kill.

"It don't seem like no good can come out of dirty work like that," muttered Happy Jack at last. "But the last I seen of the widow and the three kids they was sure a mournful lot. Suppose they're hungry tonight, with this cold. . . ." He stopped short. "Blast your soul, Sandy," he growled out, "I s'pose I'll try it. But you're going to pay some time for the murder of Jackson. I'll see to that. Now tell me what you know about the Neilan place and the folks on it. Or do you know nothing at all?"

"I know every inch of it," answered Sandy, ignoring the threat. "Ain't I scouted around that

32

place twenty times getting the lay of the land? I've had my eye on Neilan's safe for ten years, more or less. Now listen hard."

And, sitting down again in his chair, he began to talk swiftly. Happy Jack listened in gloomy silence.

III

The dinner table was a shrine of silence in the big dining room at the John Neilan house. It was a silence which Mary Thomas dreaded, always, but on this Christmas Eve it seemed to her that the silence was an accusation leveled at her head. Again and again she stole furtive glances at the stony faces of the old people. But they had no glance or word for her. Neither had they a glance or a word for each other. Their attention was fixed upon their own thoughts, and these were deadly, frozen things.

She was out of place here. Even from the first she had felt that she was out of place, since the very day when the two old folks, a dozen years before, had taken in the newly orphaned child in the hope of filling, to some extent, the vacancy formed by the loss of their son. But she had not filled it. She had only served to make the loss more visible. To be sure, they would not send her again into the world to find her own way, but, on the other hand, they could not prevent letting her see that she was ever a thorn in their sides.

And she, with the keen perception that comes to those who know grief early in life, had understood from the first and shuddered at her understanding. They never spoke cruel words. But with such silences as these they crushed her spirit time and again. When she first came, and after she learned what was wanting, she had longed many a bitter hour to change her form and face. And if wishes could change flesh, she would certainly have become like the picture of that handsome impudent-eyed boy who ever since his disappearance had remained sacred to the memory. But wishes, alas, can change neither features nor minds.

She remained the same rather pale, pretty, large-eyed girl. If she could only have had some touch of Johnny's manner. If she could at least have been a tomboy. If she could have ridden horses bareback and run and whooped about the house, she might have partly filled the niche.

In this respect she strove to change also. But she could not. She loved horses. But a bucking horse chilled her with fear. And for the rest, she was feminine of the feminine, and rather more demure than the average. The more she fought against herself, the more she became like herself. And she knew that, as she grew older, the rancher and his wife were more and more tormented by her presence.

They insisted on giving her a good education. Sometimes she thought it was because they wished to get her out of the way in this manner. But during vacation times she had to return home. And those vacations were such things of dread that they gave her nights of tearful, wakeful anticipation.

But of all vacation times Christmas was the worst, and of all the Christmas vacation there was nothing to match the horror of Christmas Eve. For on that night, whenever the eyes of the old folks fell on her, they twitched away sharply, as though in pain. She was too gentle of heart to blame them for it. She knew that, since the boy left, their lives had been passed in a long winter of despair.

Even John Neilan's own wealth was a torment to the rancher. He was still saving, but it was merely the effect of habit. Why build a fortune to which no one could fall heir except a girl—a girl who would probably marry and thereby bring the Neilan fortune into the hands of a stranger? There was no other heir. And sometimes Mary Thomas felt that Neilan actually hated her because she could receive the wealth he had created. And yet he still saved his pennies, scrupulously pretending, as he drove a hard bargain or made a niggardly purchase, that it was not for his own sake, but for the sake of Johnny . . . "when the boy comes home."

How often she had heard that! "When the boy comes home." She had dreamed of it. She had seen him coming in a thousand guises, repentant, defiant, sneaking, heroic.

Chung, the sole servant in that vast house, barn-like in its silences, padded around the room, serving the plates of chicken as John Neilan carved it. And whenever his misty old eyes fell on the face of the girl they lighted a little, as though he understood and wished to give her the warmth of kindliness which she never received from the old people. But in return she dared not so much as smile with her eyes, for mirth and happiness were sins in the house of the Neilans. What smile was worth seeing save the smile of their lost boy?

Yet, when she looked down to her plate, a faint smile did come about the corners of her mouth. It was always chicken at Christmas time at the ranch. Turkey would be too much like the real festival, and there must be no reality to Christmas until that blessed day when the boy came home. Really, they were a little absurd about it. But when she looked from one to the other of those white heads, those iron-hard faces, all sense of their absurdity left her. Twelve years of constant practice had made them, so to speak, specialists in pain.

"You haven't told us much about the school this time," said Mrs. Neilan at last, by way of breaking in on that solemn quiet. She assumed a faint smile of interest while asking the question, but her eyes looked far off.

Mary sighed. "The same courses and the same teachers as last year," she said. "There isn't much new to tell about them."

"Just as many parties as ever, I guess?" John Neilan asked suddenly. "Young Harkins still calling on you?"

"Quite often."

A glance of satisfaction passed between Mr. and Mrs. Neilan, and Mary noted it shrewdly. How well she understood them, and how gross they were not to see that she understood. Their chief interest was merely to see her well married and off their hands. Young Harkins was acceptably well off, and therefore they considered him eligible. She thought back to him with a shrinking of the heart. Perhaps, someday, driven by the constant unhappiness of her life in this home, she would accept the suit of Harkins. But seeing, in vision, the meager form and the dapper ways of that brilliant youth, she could not help sighing again.

"Why don't you ask him out home some vacation time?" asked Mr. Neilan. "Why don't you do that, Mary? You got to make some return, him spending so much time and money toting you around places. Eh?"

How could she tell them that Harkins would be alternately bored and amused by this ranch life and the people of the ranch? She obviously could not say that. But doubtless Jerry Harkins would go to the ends of the earth with her if she so much as hinted that she desired his company.

"I suppose he wants to spend his vacations with his own folks. Besides, he wouldn't be at home with us. He doesn't know ranch life and ranch ways."

"Some gents are that way," observed Neilan. "They ain't got the knack of being at home no matter where they may be. Take Johnny, now. He's different. He used to be at home in every house within thirty miles of us. That was a way he had. Give him a nail to hang up his hat and a box to sit on, and he was all right any place."

Mary Thomas glanced sharply at Mrs. Neilan and saw that the old lady was trembling, but there was no stopping John Neilan. All year, every year, he was silent on the topic of topics. But on Christmas Eve and Christmas Day his tongue was loosened. But the mother never named her missing boy, perhaps because she did not share the absolute conviction of her spouse that Johnny was still alive, or because she feared that to speak cheerfully, as though confident of his return, might irritate a capricious Providence. She merely nodded to John Neilan with a wan smile and, in a trembling voice, turned the subject of the talk.

And Mary Thomas reached out suddenly, covertly, and pressed the hand of Mrs. Neilan under the cover of the tablecloth. Mrs. Neilan started and then stared at the girl as though she feared the latter had gone mad. But, understanding that the pressure of the hand was meant by way of consoling sympathy, she flushed heavily and frowned. Mary Thomas winced back into her chair. It was always this way. They fenced her out of their inner lives. In the midst of their household they kept her a stranger.

"Hush," said John Neilan suddenly.

Outside, borne strongly toward the house on the wind, came the sound of a galloping horse and the singing of a man. There was something indescribably joyous about the song. The rhythm of it matched the swing of the gallop. There was the quick-step of youth in that singing, a great, free, ringing voice that went on smoothly, hardly jarred by the gallop which carried the singer so swiftly toward the house.

"Who is that?" asked Mrs. Neilan. "Who is expected today?"

"Nobody," answered her husband. He added, pushing back his chair: "Who do you think it could be?"

The question in his voice, the wild question in his eyes, made Mrs. John Neilan turn white.

"Don't, John," she whispered. "Don't say that. Don't think that."

Mary Thomas looked from one to the other. Long as she had lived with them, she could hardly understand a grief so bitterly vital that it turned the chance-heard sound of a galloping horse and a singing traveler into a promise and a hope.

Then—they heard it indistinctly—a heavy footfall ran up the steps.

"The side steps, John," breathed Mrs. Neilan, swaying forward and steadying herself with her withered hands against the edge of the table.

And Mary remembered that in the past, Johnny had always used the side entrance.

"Wait," gasped Mr. Neilan.

And, commanded by his raised hand, they dared not draw a breath. And then—the door banged with a jingling of the outer screen. The stranger had boldly entered without knocking. He had entered from the side. He was coming, singing softly. His footfall was swift and heavy. The old flooring trembled beneath the shocks of his heels and set the glasses quivering on the table. No, that vibration was caused by the shaking hands of Mr. and Mrs. Neilan!

Suddenly the mother was strong and the father was weak.

"Listen," breathed John Neilan. "It's the old song . . . his old song, 'The Bullwacker.'"

Mary Thomas, who had hitherto pitied them for their excitement, was caught up in the contagion.

"Don't, John!" pleaded the old woman. "I can't stand it!"

He dropped into his chair and covered his face with his hands. What old hands they were, and how much they had labored, and how much they had made his own—all for the sake of that lost child. But Mrs. Neilan rose and moved swiftly around the table and went to him. There she stood, with her hand resting on the bowed head, facing the door. All at once Mary knew how pretty the withered old woman had been in her youth. And her eyes, beneath their wrinkled, puckered lids, were now as brilliant and liquid as the eyes of a girl. The door from the library opened into the hall. The singing, now boomed out at them, was hushed to a humming sound. Then came a silence, and in the silence Mary saw the knob of the dining room door turn slowly, without sound.

Her heart stopped—then bounded violently.

The door swung open, and there against the darkness of the hall appeared a tall youth of mighty shoulders, handsome in a singularly boyish way, brown as a berry, so that his eyes in contrast were a deep-sea blue.

There he stood smiling, his hat in his hand, a thin powdering of snow across the breast of his coat gleaming in the lamplight like diamond dust. The brain of Mary Thomas swirled with a hundred thoughts. Could this be he? Were those straight-looking eyes the eyes of the mischievous, untrustworthy boy of whom she had heard so many tales? Could it be that he had returned, in fact, on this day of all days?

Suddenly he was frowning.

"Why, Mother, don't you know me?"

That word removed all doubt, swept away all hesitancy to credence.

"John!" cried the mother. "It's . . . the boy! Oh, Johnny, my dear!"

What a cry it was. The long winter of grief was over and broken. The green and golden springtime of happiness had come in an instant. She ran across the room with a step as light as the step of a girl. She reached up her arms and caught them around the big fellow in the doorway, and he, as lightly as though she were a child, lifted her bodily from the floor and kissed her.

John Neilan came stumbling blindly toward them, his hand stretched out to feel his way. And then a great arm, a great brown hand, swept out and gathered in the old man. The three were a weeping, murmuring unit.

What was her place in that room or in that house? Mary rose and slipped from the dining room.

IV

In her own room she went to the window and peered forth. The night was frosty-clear. The stars were out. The trees were doubly black against that pure white of snow which, now and then, puffing up like dust, was whirled past the window, obscuring the landscape.

Truly there was never a more perfect night for a Christmas Eve. There was something wonderfully pure and honest about that great outdoors. It could not have allowed a fraud to come out of it to the house. Fraud? No, the deep-blue eyes gleaming out of that brown face were ample assurance of his honesty. And, indeed, he had come like fate. And the instant his voice was heard, had not the father guessed? Blood spoke to blood. There was something terribly moving about it all. The heaven, full of stars, was splintered with party-colored rays. She was staring up through her tears. Her dear ones could never come to her out of the night. Out of the past she gathered the few memories which had clung in her child-mind—the tender eyes of her mother, the deep voice of her father. That was all she had to take to her heart on Christmas Eve.

A light, faltering tap was heard on the door, and then Mrs. Neilan came running in. How changed she was! Joy bubbled up within her and looked out through her eyes. Was this the iron-hard woman she had known and feared? She came to Mary and passed her arm about the girl.

"John saw you leave the room, dear. He wants you to come back. And . . . oh, Mary, isn't it like a miracle? Isn't it like an answer to a prayer? Are there really fools who don't believe in a God . . . even on Christmas Day?"

"You ought to be alone with him," Mary said, "on this first night. And I think I should be alone, too."

Ordinarily the least resistance to suggestions angered Mrs. Neilan. But she was a new woman tonight and, turning the girl toward the lamp, she studied her face and the tear-dimmed eyes.

"I know," she said. "I think, I know. Poor dear! But you must come down. We have happiness enough to spare for the whole world. And why should we care about one night? He's promised that he'll never leave again. Never!"

Mary could not resist. She went down the stairs with Mrs. Neilan, their arms about each other like two friends of one age. That dark stairway had always been a place of dread to Mary, but now she felt as though she were going down into a sunshine presence.

A new place had been laid at the table, and the wanderer sat at it with a plate heaped high. He rose at once and came to them.

44

"They've told me about you a little," he said. "I figured maybe you'd think that this was just a family party, and that you were out of it. But, to my way of thinking, you're as much a part of the family as I am. Let's all sit around and be sociable, eh?"

He took her to her chair. He drew it out and seated her. Then he hurried around to his place again and attacked the ample provisions that Mrs. Neilan had heaped before him. And what a time followed! How the father heaped questions—how the mother warded those questions away until her boy should have eaten. And eat he did with tremendous appetite. He talked as he could in the brief interludes.

"Where have I been? Everywhere! North, but mostly south. What have I been doing? Everything! Remember I was a work hater? Well, I've had to swing a pick and a shovel and hammer a drill. I've had to pitch hay and mow it and stack it. I've had to feed on a baler. I've roped and branded and bored fence holes and strung wire. Look there!"

He extended his long arms so that they dominated the whole table—what a huge fellow he was, thought Mary—and, turning his palms uppermost, he exposed to their view hands callused from the heel of the palm to the work-squared tips of the fingers. And as he flexed them, the big wrist cords stood out, mute testimony to lifting of weights and struggling at burdens.

"Poor boy! Poor Johnny!" his mother said, and sighed.

"Poor nothing!" The wanderer grinned with an irrepressible smile of good humor. "It's been a twelve-year lark. I've had to work, sure enough . . . but those calluses are the price of freedom. By the way, I figure there's no price too high to pay for that."

"John," murmured Mrs. Neilan. "Johnny, dear, do you mean that?"

"Oh, no fear of me slipping off again," he said, flushing a little. "I've had my fling, right enough. What you see, Dad?"

The old man had taken the right hand of the newcomer and now examined it earnestly.

"The other hand is tolerable pale from glove wearing," he said slowly, "but this one looks as though they ain't been many gloves on it, Son." Raising his eyes gravely, he added, as he relinquished the hand: "I dunno where you been, but around these parts you may remember that gents that don't wear gloves on their right hands keep 'em bare for one reason . . . and that was so's they'd be quick and clean on the draw."

"John!" cried Mrs. Neilan to her husband. "You have no right to accuse Johnny of being a fighting man. And on his first night home."

"I've done my share of fighting," said the

wanderer, his face darkening slightly as he looked down to the sun-browned right hand that was now the center of the conversation. "I don't deny that I've had my troubles, and I guess I have to admit that I ain't been in the habit of running away from fights. But"—and here he raised his head and looked around with a suddenly bright smile—"I can say this much . . . I've never picked on any gent on the ranges, north or south. I've never forced a fight. I've never hunted trouble. And I've never taken an unfair advantage. If what you're driving at is that maybe some think I'm a gunfighter, well, I got to admit that I've been called that. But I've never used a gun to get a gent that hadn't done me a wrong or wronged a pal of mine. I've never used it to get something that wasn't mine by rights. Does that clear me up?"

And he looked a straight challenge at John Neilan. The latter laughed softly and joyously.

"Do you think I expected you to turn out a softy?" he asked. "Do you think I expected you to turn out a ladies' man? Ain't you John Neilan's son?"

Here the door from the hall opened, and the servant, who had been absent from the dining room for some time, now stood grinning and nodding before them.

Mrs. Neilan rose at once with a flush of pleasure. "Chung has something to show us," she

47

suggested. "Let's see what it is. You first tonight, Johnny."

The big fellow stepped smilingly ahead, crossed the dark gap of the hallway, and passed on through the open doors of the parlor. It was a flare of light from the huge lamp that hung in chains from the center of the ceiling, and from three or four more big circular burners placed most effectively to cast their light on one corner. And in that corner stood a young fir tree, with gay trimming heaped upon its branches, and all about it on the floor was a jumble of wrapped-up boxes and packages. Some of the paper on those packages had yellowed with time, others were fresh and crisp. It was a huge pile, spread wide across the floor.

"What in the world!" exclaimed the wanderer.

"It's twelve Christmases all in one," said the mother, with a trembling voice. "See what's here, Johnny. Open them for him, Dad. No, give them to him to open!"

"Here's the first one," said the old man, quickly making a selection. "I remember getting it. More'n twelve years ago. Here you are Johnny!"

And he thrust a long, slender, heavy box into the hands of a stranger.

Mary Thomas glanced to the big youth with an expectant smile, but her smile went out. He, too, was attempting to smile, but his face was white and his mouth pinched in at the sides.

"You been remembering me every Christmas since I . . . left?"

"Remembering you? Son, have we remembered anything but you?"

"Open it, dear," said the mother. "Open it."

The big hand strayed slowly down the length of the package. Anyone could guess from the shape and weight that it was a gun.

But instead of opening it, he repeated slowly: "Every Christmas?"

"Aye, every one."

"It's been twelve years," the big man said huskily, "and that's a long time to wait. I ain't written to you. I've treated you plumb bad all the way through. And still . . . every year . . . for twelve years . . . you ain't forgot me a single time at Christmas."

"Open up them packages and see," John Neilan said eagerly. "Ah, Johnny, it's been a sad business, getting presents every year and never knowing if you . . ."

"I knew," said Mrs. Neilan suddenly. "I always knew he'd come."

But Mary Thomas heard their voices no more distinctly than if they had been ghost whispers. She saw nothing but the face of the wanderer, gray and drawn with pain.

"I didn't know," he muttered, "that fathers and mothers could be like this. I didn't know what Christmas could be."

"You didn't have much cause to find out from me," said the father. "I treated you pretty bad, Son. I was too busy making money and stacking it away to pay much attention to my own boy. But I've learned different in these twelve years. I know now what's worthwhile in the world. You remember what we had the last trouble about? About the key to the safe?" He laughed in excitement. "The safe is in the cellar in the old place, and here's that key to the lock. Take it, Johnny, and keep it for me, and if you want everything in the safe, go and take it and don't ask no questions. Money? Money's dirt compared to having you back."

The wanderer accepted the key with a trembling hand, and then offered to return it. "Too much trust is like too much liquor," he said. "You sure you want me to have this? You sure it ain't going to turn my head for me?"

"That's only the beginning," declared the father. "What you do with things don't matter. They're yours. Now open the packages, Son!"

"Not now," said the stranger slowly. "Not now. Seems to me the way used to be to open up things on Christmas morning. Ain't that right? I . . . I'll open 'em up then, all together."

But for some reason Mary Thomas knew, as she watched him, that he would never break the string on one of those packages. Instinct told her that, and she wondered at it.

V

In all that followed throughout the evening, Happy Jack was aware of one thing only, and that was the watchful eye of Mary Thomas. Whatever he was doing, she caught him with a glance now and then, and it seemed to the big fellow from the southland that the steady eyes looked through and through him and found out his guilty secret.

In the meantime, fresh tides of life and uproarious noise began to invade the house. From the cheerless bunkhouse, where they were drowsing on this unhappy Christmas Eve, most melancholy of all nights to the wanderers, the cowpunchers of the Neilan outfit were roused and brought to the big house itself—an unprecedented act of hospitality on the part of the rancher, for since the disappearance of Johnny hardly half a dozen strangers had succeeded in getting past the door of the house.

They came haltingly, prepared to find it a false invitation which Chung had extended to them. But they found, instead of a chilling reception, open arms! Mrs. John Neilan with color as high as a girl of eighteen floated here and there among them, making them at home. And Mary Thomas, with fewer words, was an even more effective worker. The resources of the kitchen were called upon. The big dining table was spread again. From the depths of the cellar heavily cobwebbed bottles of sherry—how long, long ago they had been stored there and for twelve years been untouched—were brought up. One by one they disappeared. It was like turning a hose on the desert, save that the dry throats of the cowboys gave some return. They opened in song. They toasted old John Neilan until even his hard eyes began to twinkle. And they gave a tremendous rouse for the returned prodigal. And then they all stood up and sang for Mary Thomas and drank to her. It was a very great occasion. It was an evening when no one could remember anything that was said. But all were riotously happy.

Gifts were found for all. One robust cowpuncher received a fine revolver, another a watch, another a saddle—and so on until everyone had his share. This was wild liberality, but old John Neilan cared not for possessions on such a night as this.

"The old boy's gone mad," one of the punchers observed.

"Nope, he's just woke up and come to his senses," insisted a second. "This is the way he would've growed to be if the kid hadn't walked off in the old days. Now he's making up for lost time. What do you think of the kid?"

"Why, I figure he'd be a tolerable good partner, and a tolerable bad one to have for an enemy.

You seen old Chip step on his toe a while back?"

"Nope. What about it?"

"Nothing happened. But just for a second Johnny Neilan give Chip a bad look. And he sure swings an ugly eye, I'll tell a man. Like a bull terrier that just walks up and sinks a tooth into your leg without letting out a growl. Look there! The kid may have wandered around a lot, but I think he's found a home, eh?"

This last remark was caused by an earnest, head-to-head conversation which was taking place between Happy Jack and Mary Thomas. Certainly the wanderer evinced a great and growing interest in the girl. As for Mary Thomas, her color had risen. She was talking with animation and laughter, and a rather grim smile of appreciation played around the lips of Happy Jack.

The dinner for the cowboys was now breaking up. They were comparing the gifts which the old man had brought out for them. They were exchanging yarns and slaps on the back and guffawing hugely at nothing in particular. Someone had brought in an armful of fir boughs and scattered them here and there at random, so that the air breathed with the resinous scent that means Christmas.

"Hey, Chip Flinders!" called one of the two whose comments have just been noticed. "Hey, Chip!"

An oldish fellow with hair dull gray at the temples and a weather-worn face paused near them. "What's biting you?" he asked, without a smile.

"There ain't any cloud in the sky except you, Chip. What's wrong?"

Chip Flinders regarded his questioner without pleasure. "Don't you see nothing wrong?" he asked at last.

"Nope."

"Have you took a look at Johnny Neilan?"

"A pile of 'em, and he looks like something that's all right to me."

"Does he? Maybe he is. I dunno. But he reminds me powerful of somebody that ain't all right."

"Who?"

"I dunno. That's what I'm figuring on and trying to remember . . . where I seen him before with a gun in each hand and . . ." He wandered on, his head down, his face thoughtful.

"Huh," grunted one of the pair who had asked the questions. "What if the kid has done some fighting. Is that ag'in' him? If fighting is so plumb bad, old Chip himself had ought to watch out. He's done his share in the south, they say."

"Yep, and he bears the marks of it. I've seen him stripped. All chawed up like as if a mountain lion had wrestled with him."

But there was no other blot on the good cheer

54

of the occasion. Only the frown of Chip darkened the affair until the hour of midnight was turned and Christmas Day itself was ushered in with a ringing carol.

After that they broke up quickly, and, while the people of the house went to their rooms, the cowpunchers returned to the bunkhouse with broad grins of content, each man with the warmth of sherry in his blood and Christmas in his mind and a gift in his hand. Only Chip Flinders stared gloomily down at the snow over which he was striding.

From the window of the room to which John Neilan had led him, Happy Jack looked down at the procession of the cowpunchers with a frown as dark as the frown of Chip. For he, too, was striving with all his might to remember where he had seen that face with the tufts of gray hair above the temples and the solemn, worn expression. But he could not remember. The harder he concentrated the more his mind went adrift from the past, and when he felt that he had discovery under his mental fingertips, an image from this gay and crowded evening would flit across his eyes and obscure the past.

At length Happy Jack turned away, as the last of the cowpunchers disappeared through the door of the bunkhouse and looked about the room. It needed only a glance to make sure that this was the only room where Johnny Neilan had slept in the old days. From the wall a huge, dim enlargement of a photograph looked down at him, showing a youth with faintly smiling lips and a twinkle of mischief in the eyes. Even in the picture of the boy there was a startling resemblance to Happy Jack. No doubt if Johnny Neilan had lived to maturity, he would have been sufficiently different, but in his childhood he possessed the promise of all the features of Happy Jack. It was not strange that the sharp eye of Sandy Crisp had marked the resemblance and taken advantage of it.

Sandy Crisp! What a devil incarnate he was!

Thinking of the outlaw, Happy Jack moved about the room making what discoveries he could. And there were plenty of things to interest him. He found in the bureau drawers heaps of undergarments, and dozens of socks, some worn and neatly darned, some fresh—the equipment of Johnny Neilan, no doubt. In a big closet, large as a little room by itself, he found a great assortment of guns and fishing tackle on one side and articles for riding on the other side—bridles and spurs and saddle blankets. Truly, the boy had been given enough things to amuse himself. What had caused the discontent that eventually drove him from the house?

As though to answer him, at the moment his hand brushed aside the curtain from a little row of bookshelves, and there he found row on row of textbooks. There was a Latin grammar and a tattered commentaries. There was a copy of *Classic Myths* and a translation of the *Iliad*. And so, on and on, Happy Jack picked up book after book, all unfamiliar to him as strange faces in a strange land. Had poor young Johnny Neilan been forced to struggle through all these?

He opened them. The interiors presented page after page filled with crude drawings of bucking horses and guns. These had formed the occupation of young Neilan when he was supposed to be imbibing knowledge. And beyond a doubt this was the nightmare that had driven him away from the ranch and north on the endless trail of adventure until he died there on the log jam, laughing and waving his hat. No doubt he had been a wild youth. But perhaps there had been little harm in his wildness. Had he grown up, he might have done things as fine and brave as his death scene, and far more useful.

Happy Jack was hard enough. For there are few, unfortunately, who acquire such calluses of labor on their hands without getting similar calluses about the heart. But, sitting in this room, the presence of the dead boy was around him like a ghost, rattling at the fishing tackle in the closet or handling the guns or humming in the wind that now curled around the corner of the house in a steady gale.

A foolish insistence on the study of books had

driven young Neilan away from his home. And did not the father deserve the pains which had come to him? He was a hard man. There was no doubt of that. Sandy Crisp had said so with profound conviction. And had not Happy himself watched the painful intentness with which the rancher followed the raising of each glass of his precious sherry? One large and kindly impulse had induced that sacrifice of good liquor, but it seemed that the old fellow sighed at once because of his own generosity. Hard he certainly was, and though the return of his son, as if from the grave, had loosened his spirit, might it not be a kindliness of the moment only and no permanent change? And, indeed, even in that happiness there was a selfish motive. John Neilan had acquired someone to whom he could leave his property. Hence he rejoiced.

In the meantime, Happy Jack held the key to the safe.

He drew out the key and then the plan of the house with which Sandy Crisp had furnished him. He glanced over it to make sure that he had every winding of hall and stairway in mind. Yes, it would be perfectly simple to steal down the back stairs and into the basement and return the same way, then make his exit through the window of his room and over the roof of the verandah to the freedom of the snow beyond. To slip out to the stables with his loot, saddle his horse, and then ride to the rendezvous in the neighboring woods where Crisp waited—that would be a simple thing.

Happy Jack stood up, resolved to act. So doing, his glance fell full on the eye of the boy in the photograph, and Happy shrank back with a curse.

For a moment he wavered, the good and the evil fighting in him for mastery. But it has been said that Happy had elements of hardness in his nature, and he showed it now. On the one hand he was betraying a trust for the first time in his life. On the other hand he was securing a stake—for young Jackson's family even more than himself, it's true—for the first time in his life. He made a rough accounting between right and wrong, as he stood there scowling at the image of the true Johnny Neilan.

To be sure, this was a scoundrelly thing to do. But had not other men done scoundrelly things to him? How many hundreds—aye, thousands—of dollars had he not loaned to friends? And how many cents on the dollar had been returned to him?

He had gone through life giving with both hands, not only of money but of his personal services. He had not pried into the right and wrong of the requests that were made of him. Out of a whole heart he had done his best to meet every demand. The result was that he found himself past twenty-five without a cent in the world—with no possessions except his horse and gun.

What was the result of all of this reasoning? Why, simply that the world owed him something for what he had given the world. He wanted both principal and interest back and, if he got it from Neilan, what was wrong? It was only a fair exchange, taking from a man who really had not a need for his money.

It was certainly a tortuous course of reasoning such as has led to many a crime being committed. But when he concluded the silent argument, it must be said in favor of Happy that his forehead was cold and wet with perspiration, so that he growled: "Maybe I'm losing my nerve."

That decided him. He tightened his belt, looked to his gun, and saw that it came easily from the holster under his touch, then he advanced to the door of his room, opened it an inch or more, and listened.

VI

There was a hall light burning, a pendent lamp which, with the wick turned low, cast a dim, yellowish haze up and down the corridor, only bright where it fell on the red carpet in a circle around the black shadow of the bowl. The walls advanced and receded in faintly glowing yellow-gray, and every doorway, sunk into the thick, old walls of the house, was a gaping depth of black. Happy Jack peered up and down this gloomy tunnel and then listened to the faint thudding of his heart against his ribs.

He had read in stories and he had heard in tales about the campfire of men hearing the beating of the heart in moments of fear, but in all the battles which had marked his stormy life he had never known it before. Danger, to him, had been something to be greeted as a friend rather than an enemy, a thing to rush at with extended arms, even if those arms ended in clenched fists. But this new emotion, this fear, was a stranger to him, and he wondered at himself.

He was continually compressing his lips to swallow, but his dry throat refused to obey. And his fingers trembled on the doorknob, in sign of the tremor of the nerves all through his big body. He hardly knew himself in this great, shaken hulk of flesh.

The thought came to him that his crime would be discovered as soon as the morning came. He closed the door to the hall and leaned heavily against it, panting. His thoughts wrestled him to and fro, the perspiration still streaming down his face. If only this money were to be gained by facing some actual danger. But no, there was no one in the house to fight. An old woman and a young one, and a man well past his fighting days.

They were the only ones to face him. His enemy was shame, fierce and biting shame. Suppose that fresh-faced, clear-eyed girl, Mary Thomas, should spy him out, should look in on him as, with guilty hands, he opened the door of the safe and took out the greenbacks.

He found himself staring at the wall like one stricken with the sight of a ghost. But this was all perfectly childish. He must go down at once. At once! The world owed the money to him.

Suddenly he was through the door and out in the hall. He advanced now very steadily, finding his progress much easier after he took the first step. The start was the hard part. In the meantime, the boards of the flooring creaked terribly under his feet. Strange that they had been so silent when he came upstairs to his bed just a few minutes before. But dread and horror of the thing which he was about to do sharpened his perceptions, and a murmur of board rubbing against board that could hardly have been heard a yard away seemed to Happy Jack loud enough to waken every person in the house.

And had they not been wakened? Was not that the sound of someone sitting up in bed, the springs creaking under the shifted weight? And was not that the thudding of a guarded footfall approaching a door nearby? And was not that the rattle of a lock on which a hand had fallen?

No, it was only a straying draft that had shaken

the door, but for a moment he paused, frozen with fear. When he went on again, he was shaking like a leaf—he, Happy Jack, famous through the southland as the hero of the Morgan Run fight. But now he was unnerved.

The creaking of the boards in the upper hall was nothing compared with the noises that accompanied him down the stairs. They literally swayed and reeled beneath him. They groaned from end to end under his descending weight. It seemed as though the dead timber of the house were living and attempting to warn the inhabitants of the dastardly crime about to be committed by this trusted guest, this false son of the family.

Such fancies made play in the brain of Happy Jack, and each one of them was almost a real possibility. He gave each a serious consideration until he felt, before he reached the bottom of the steps, that he should go mad.

But there he was in the great open rooms of the lower floor. In a far corner, barely visible against the dim square of a window, stood the Christmas tree, like a gaunt ghost holding out arms. Happy Jack caught up a hand against his eyes and shut out the reproachful vision.

He returned down the hall to the rear of the house, opened the door which, on his plan, was jotted down as the entrance to the cellar, and found himself staring down into utter darkness.

He took out the little electric lantern with which Sandy Crisp had thoughtfully provided him and snapped a small torrent of light that tumbled down the damp steps and showed brown-black dirt below.

Then he went down, cursing the squeaking boards with each step, next blessing the muffling dirt under his heels. He found the safe room easily. Certainly Sandy Crisp must have studied the house in the most minute detail, just as he had said.

"Go in blindfold," he had declared, "and I'll give you a plan so good that you can feel your way around and come to the right place."

The safe was kept in a room walled off by itself. The walls were of foundation stones, each one of huge dimensions and solidly mortared together; the great door was adorned with a tremendous padlock, a device such as Happy had never seen before. Double-fold idiot that he was. Sandy had warned him to get the key to the padlock as well as the key to the safe.

Suddenly he breathed a sigh of relief. He could not get that key tonight. He would go out and tell Sandy that the deal was off, and that he wanted to have no more to do with it. No, that would send Sandy abroad with a huge tale about the weak nerve of Happy Jack—how he started out to do a robbery and lacked the courage to carry it through.

As a matter of fact, a crime once started was as good as completed, so far as one's own conscience went. So argued unhappy Jack as he stood staring at the padlock. Automatically, not with a hope, he tried the safe key in the padlock. At the first turn something yielded. Astonished, he turned it again, and behold, the lock was sprung!

Happy Jack blinked. But, after all, it was perfectly clear. The rancher had simply ordered a padlock that would duplicate the lock of his safe.

The door now began to swing open without the pressure of his hand, and presently Happy sent the shaft of light from his torch straight into the face of a big, squat safe, older than three generations of men. The lock on the door and the lock on the safe had been too implicitly trusted by the old man for, once an expert cracksman got at the safe, with even a can opener, the safe would be gutted of its money.

To Jack, of course, it was a very simple affair. In half a minute the door of the safe was open, and he was pulling out drawer after drawer. The one was piled with documents, another was crammed with account books, and in the third he found the money. When his fingers closed over it, he waited for the exultant leap of his pulses, but it did not come. He did not pause to count but, glancing at the denominations of a few of the bills and then estimating the thickness of the pile, he figured it to be between thirty and forty thousand dollars.

Why did the rancher keep so much money on the ranch? Was it because, miser-like, he loved to sun himself in the presence of hard cash?

A door slammed heavily. Happy Jack whirled with the speed of guilt, which is swifter by far than the speed of a striking snake, and his gun was in his hand as he whirled. But in a moment he knew that the door had banged somewhere in an upper story of the house. He was safe, unobserved as yet.

He felt a sudden panic, a blind, strange thing spring on him out of the thin air and cling to him like a writhing, living object. Danger was all about him. It was grinning at him from the shadows. It was lurking beyond the door!

Not stopping to close and relock the door to the safe, Happy pocketed the cash, and sneaked out to the door of the little room and crouched there, shooting flashes of light from side to side and combing the cellar to make sure that no one was watching and waiting.

Then he cursed himself for his stupidity. What was so likely as the light itself to attract attention? He snapped it out and started at a run for the stairway leading to the floor above. As though in key with his emotions, a terrific gale at the same time smashed against the house and howled about the corners, wailing and shaking doors and windows. And in that wild uproar, springing through the darkness, Happy Jack reached the staircase and flew to the top.

He was through the door, shut it quickly behind him, and then leaned against it to shut behind the danger that seemed to have snapped at his heels and barely missed him as he darted through to safety. And his heart, all the time, worked like a trip hammer. The violence of its actions shook him.

Ten seconds more, and he would be through the door, outside, and on his way. What should prevent him? He pulled the hat lower on his forehead and looked up and down. The house was quiet. The wind had fallen. Sudden calm was everywhere. And Happy stepped quickly to the front door of the house.

With his hand on the knob he paused, remembering that he had taken off his coat and left it in the room above. But what difference did the coat make?

He began to open the door, and yet he closed it again without stepping out. The coat made every difference, now that he came to think of it. As long as he was committing burglary, he should do it both boldly and smoothly. And to run out like a frightened child in his shirt sleeves—certainly that would bring a smile to the sinister eyes of Sandy Crisp.

On so small a thing the fate of Happy Jack

was hanging. One step through the door and he was committed forever to a life of crime. But if he turned back—who could tell? He was not yet entirely across the borderline of the law, perhaps.

He went up the stairs more swiftly than he had come down. Now that the matter had been pushed so close to completion, he would brazen it through the last stages with a rush. In his room again, he caught up the coat and shoved his arms into the sleeves, leaving it unbuttoned, for in that manner he was given a freer play at his revolver butt.

Again he hesitated, in the act of stepping from the room. Would it not be better to leave something as a message?

He tore a flyleaf out of a book and leaned over it to scribble a note, but, while he searched for words, a gust of wind from the open window flicked the paper from under his fingers and tossed it to the floor. He scooped it up with an oath and found lying before him, printed on the leaf: *The New Testament.*

Happy Jack crunched the paper to a ball, while he drew his breath in a deep intake. That was the book of Christ, and this was Christ's day! His hand, swinging back against the pocket of the coat, struck the package of greenbacks, and he jerked his arm wide again, cursing. Fate was against him.

Well, he would get clear of this house. It was

beginning to weigh on him with a mortal burden, even the necessity of being under its roof. He turned to the door, in time to hear two light knocks upon it.

The sound stopped his heartbeat.

It was utter folly, of course. What had he to fear from any creature who announced his coming and did not strike him by surprise?

"Come in!" called Happy Jack.

There was no answer. Then he knew that his throat had refused to give body to the words he tried to speak. He went to the door and drew it open, and white against the darkness of the hall, he found himself looking down into the face of his pseudo-mother, Mrs. John Neilan.

VII

She was wrapped to the throat in a black dressing gown, and her white hair, quite disordered, floated like a mist about her face. But, at the sight of Happy Jack, her eyes brightened.

"You," said Happy Jack. "You?"

He would rather have faced the guns of ten hard fighters at that moment than the pair of eyes that one glimpse of him had so brightened. Suddenly she was clinging to him.

"Johnny!" she was pleading. "You're not going?"

"Me?" muttered Happy Jack. "Me? Why should I go?"

"Your hat and your coat . . . at this hour . . ."

"I couldn't sleep. Being all sort of filled up with happiness about being home, I thought I'd step out and take a walk in the snow to get quieted down again. You see?"

She stroked his big arm gently, as though to make sure of him by the sense of touch, not trusting her eyes or ears.

"And that's all?" she pleaded.

"Yes."

She drew back at that, laughing a little. "I guess I'm a goose," she said, "but I haven't been able to sleep, either. Do you know what I've been doing? I've been standing at the window, half expecting, any minute, to see you slip out and go to the stable for your horse. You see, when you talked about the freedom of being your own master in the world, the idea stayed with me. And I didn't see how you could be happy here with us. And then . . . then I came up to make sure of you." She laughed again, but this time happily.

"And here I am," said Happy Jack, wretched to the bottom of his heart as he studied the aged, kindly face. No matter what charges could be brought against Neilan, there was nothing to be said against his wife. And in the final accounting, how black would be the record of his trick upon this woman. "Here I am, and here to stay."

He forced a smile to cover the lie and give it reality.

"And happy, dear?"

"Aye," said Happy Jack. "I'm happy."

"When you opened the door you fairly growled at me. 'You' you said, and in such a voice. As though I were an armed man, you know. And, Johnny, won't you take off that hat and coat for just a minute? It makes me nervous to see you dressed to go."

He obeyed without a word and turned to find her nodding and smiling.

"When you were a boy, dear," she said, "you'd have growled at me for being so foolish."

"Was I as bad as that?"

"Not bad. Oh, no. But just headstrong. I suppose every boy with the makings of a man in him is that way now and then. But you remember the checked suit I bought for your birthday, the one you burned because you were ashamed to wear it? That was one of the things I couldn't understand in the old days. But, oh, Johnny, how much more I can understand now."

"Did I do that?" muttered Happy Jack. "Did I burn the suit? The one you gave me for a birthday present?"

"But don't tell me you've forgotten! It was your thirteenth birthday, you know. The last one . . ."

She stopped, and her eyes filled. And Happy

Jack threw back his head and opened his shirt at the throat. He was stifling. What would go on in the brain and the soul of the woman when she learned of the hoax that had been played?

"I remember," he said huskily.

"And now you're angry because I've brought it up. I didn't mean to . . ."

"Hush," gasped Happy Jack. "Don't talk like that. Angry? With you? Do you know where a gent like me ought to be when he's talking to a lady like you? Down on his knees. Down on his knees, thinking what a mean, sneaking coyote he is."

She ran to him and stopped him with a raised forefinger. "That isn't a bit like my Johnny," she said. "I . . . I'm afraid you've had hard times, or you'd never have learned to talk like this."

"I was a brute of a hard-mouthed kid," Happy Jack said. "All I knew was pulling on the bit. But I've learned different. It was kicked into me."

"Who dared to strike you?"

"About a hundred, off and on"—Happy chuckled—"have taken a crack at me."

"My dear, my dear," murmured the mother. "But I have you safely home now."

Happy Jack laughed. "I've growed big enough to . . . to take care of myself tolerable well," he declared. "But . . ."

He stopped. She had uttered a little cry of horror and, reaching up, she pushed back his shirt and exposed his chest. A great ragged scar ran across it. And, drawing back the cloth a little more, she saw a broad spot, shining like silver.

"Johnny!" she gasped. "What . . . what made those marks on you?"

"Them?" Happy Jack said carelessly, but rebuttoning his shirt, nevertheless. "Well, you see, I've had little mixes now and then. And those are the marks."

"But on your chest . . . weren't you nearly killed?"

"Pretty near, a couple of times. But I come through, all right."

"And that's the world you called your world of freedom. A world of death is what it is!"

"Maybe. But, when a gent's knocking around, he's got to take what comes his way."

"Tell me this minute," demanded the mother, "the names of the . . . the creatures who hurt you like that."

"The long one," said Happy thoughtfully, "with the fancy lace-work about the edges, that scar come from a little run-in I had with a horse. Him and me had it out to see which was the better man. And he put me to bed. He got me off the saddle by running under a tree. And when I was down, he come along and done a dance on top of me."

She covered her eyes, shuddering. "And they killed the horrible brute, I hope."

"Killed him? Killed old Captain?" He started, almost in alarm, and then relaxed in a chuckle. "I should say not. Captain is the horse I ride, and there's none better. He can turn around on a dime and jump like he has wings and dodge like a yearling calf. Besides, him and me are pals."

Mrs. Neilan looked at him as though he stood at a great distance and she had to peer hard to make him out.

"I never could understand in the old days," she said sadly, "and I guess I'll have to give up trying to understand now. But I'll never give up loving you, Johnny, and keeping you. And . . . and that long straight scar below the ragged one, dear?"

"It don't make no pretty story," said Happy Jack. "But I'll tell you if it'll make you feel any easier. I was playing poker one night in a strange town with some strange gents. Playing poker with strangers is like eating in a strange cook house. You got to keep watching your hand or you'll starve. Anyway, there was a Canuck down from Canada with a disposition like a branding-fire on a hot day. He was so plumb nacheral mean that he cussed his tobacco while he was rolling a cigarette, and he cussed the cigarette after the tobacco was in it, and he cussed the match while he was lighting the cigarette, and then he wound up by cussing the floor he dropped the match on. You know that kind?

"Well, he was sure a fine gent to sit across the table from at poker. If you made a bet against him, he looked at you like he was picking out the place where he was going to shoot you. He had me plumb nervous with his little ways and his hitching at a knife one minute and playing with a gun the next. Anyway, to make a short yarn of it, I come over three kings and a brace of Jacks in his hand with three bullets and a pair of measly little deuces in mine. And I pretty near cleaned him out. Well, he sure went up in smoke. He was trembling all over, he was so mad. He passed a word or two at me, and then he reaches over the table with a grin and says he'll shake hands to show there're no hard feelings. And when he had my right hand, he pulls a knife with his left and slashes me. That's the way that happened."

"I hope they lynched him!" Mrs. Neilan gritted through her teeth, her eyes shining with anger.

"Nope, they took him to a hospital. I took care not to kill him, but I sure salted him away plenty. And the funny part was that it took all my winnings at that game to pay his hospital expenses."

"You paid them?"

"Think I was going to leave him to charity? Nope. I have my fun and pay my bills for it. I guess that's all you want to know about the scars?"

"I . . . I'm afraid to ask any more, Johnny. But

there's a round, white one, about the size of a twenty-five-cent piece . . ."

"That was at Morgan Run. They got me good that day."

"Who are they?"

"I was doing a favor for a friend of mine that was a sheriff down south. Not that I play in with posses much. But a gang turned loose and did a couple of pretty bad jobs around the country. When they robbed a house, they burned it afterward to cover their tracks. And that ain't a pretty game. So I rode in the sheriff's party, and we took up with 'em at Morgan Run."

"And then . . . ?" she breathed.

"Then there was quite a little party, and they nicked me plenty. But we got 'em all."

"I want to know."

"You'll never know from me," he said gloomily. "That's something I don't talk about. It . . . it's the only day in my life that I shot to kill. But the skunks got me cornered, and it was me or them. They didn't leave no other choice, and I had to work quick. But here I am, and their trails are all a blank. It was a bad day."

Mrs. John Neilan stared at him in profound wonder.

"And to think," she whispered, "that once I held all of you in my arms . . . so easily . . . so easily . . . Johnny, are you happy to be back with us here?"

"Don't I look it?"

"You have such big, fierce ways." The mother sighed as she spoke. "Sometimes even your own mother is afraid of you."

"Heaven rest her! Do you think she is?"

"What do you mean?" asked Mrs. Neilan, worried.

"Nothing. But you're not really afraid?"

"I suppose not . . . really. Until you begin to talk about battles."

"You asked me, you know."

"I'll have to keep on asking you until I know about every one, but they won't be twice-told tales for me, Johnny. Only, I have to hear everything once. Because everything that you've done is a part of you. And everything that's a part of you is a part of me. And I have to understand myself, don't I?"

He chuckled at her reasoning.

"But will you prove you're happy here?"

"Any way I can."

"By making me a great gift?"

"It's Christmas," Happy Jack said, "and that's the time for giving, I guess."

"Then promise me, dear, that you'll never again draw a weapon on any human being. Life is not worth being bought at the expense of another's life. Will you promise? Besides, I'm going to wall you about with such fences of peace that you'll never need a gun again. Will you promise, and make your old mother happy?"

"I promise," said Happy Jack. After all, what did one more lie matter?

"Heaven bless you for it. Now I'll go back to my bed and sleep . . . the first real sleep in twelve years, my dear."

VIII

When she was gone, Happy Jack sank inertly into a chair. He remembered once having encountered a formidable enemy in a battle in which no shot was fired. But they merely passed and repassed each other half a dozen times in the little cattle town that day, and always when they were near there was a steady exchange of side glances and insulting smiles. That night the other had ridden suddenly out of town and, when word of his going was brought to Happy Jack by an attentive friend who knew the secret of the feud, Happy had collapsed on a chair as though from the exhaustion of a twenty-hour ride.

So it was now. Every nerve in his body seemed frayed by the strain of talking to Mrs. Neilan. And on his lips was still the tingle of the kiss with which she had left him. It was a living evidence of his lie. It was a brand for his guilt. Never again could he raise his head as an honest man and look his fellows in the face.

How it came about, Happy Jack was never to know. But it was as though a light were turned on in his brain and suddenly he was seeing everything clearly. He had raised his head and met, accidentally, the eyes of the boy pictured on the wall. And he knew as he examined those mischievous eyes that what he intended to do this night was exactly what the dead son would have done had he lived. Yes, it had been fortunate indeed that he had not lived, for surely he would have broken the heart of his mother and maddened his father. That episode of the burned birthday suit, and all it connoted of sullen pride and silly vanity, had not been thrown away upon Happy Jack. And, searching the face for signs of other weaknesses, he was not long in finding them. The eyes were too close together. The mouth was too loose, even for boyhood, and without promise of refinement. Such a daring deed of bravado as he had enacted on the day of his death in the log jam, that face was certainly capable of promising. But for any tenderness, generosity, faith, there was no room.

He, Happy Jack, the man without a name, without a family, without a past save that of his own making, was beyond all shadow of question the better man of the two. This stealing in the night, this shameful imposture upon two old people, would have been in the line of the capabilities of the dead man. He, Happy Jack, was above it. He took from his pocket the thick bundle of bills. And he ran his fingers over them. Every one of them represented the wages that might be earned by a month or more of hard labor. Here, in his grip, was the cash valuation of two or three lifetimes of work, for himself and that widow and her three children. All in the grip of his one hand!

He flung it from him to the top of the bureau. He tore out another flyleaf, this time taking a little more care in the selection of the book to be mutilated, and he scrawled across the paper:

This is why I came, and the reason I'm leaving it behind me is because of I don't know what. But I'm not Johnny. You can lay to that. And I'm a pile sorry for having got up a lot of hopes that are not true.

Yours to the end of time,

Happy Jack

And when the thing was done, he drew a great breath of relief. After all, it was a marvelously simple thing to do. Once he set his hand to it. It seemed to him that a hand fell from his shoulder, the invisible hand of Sandy Crisp which had impelled him first toward this cruel and wicked crime, and which had kept urging him on.

He remembered another thing out of the evening, something which at the time he had taken lightly enough, but which now loomed larger and larger in importance. It was his promise to Mrs. Neilan that he would never again draw his gun upon a human being. Great beads of sweat stood out on his forehead as he thought of it. And that he, Happy Jack, of all people should have made such a promise. It was madness. It was worse—it was suicide! A hundred men would welcome an opportunity to take him at a disadvantage and shoot to kill. Happy Jack without a gun? They would come flocking at the news like buzzards gathering above a dying bull.

Slowly he wiped off the perspiration. His own image from the mirror above the bureau looked forth at him, and he saw a drawn, anguished face.

And, as a matter of fact, he was confident that he was signing his death warrant as he drew out his Colt and placed it on the paper and the money below the paper. Mrs. Neilan would understand when she saw it. At least she would understand what a thousand good men in the southland could have told her before—that the word of Happy Jack was as good as gold.

Once more he turned toward the door of the room, and this time he passed through it, walking strangely light without the weight of the gun at his hip. But there was no other way. To be sure, once outside the house he would have to run the gantlet of Sandy Crisp and whatever men Sandy might have with him. But, if he wished to keep

81

his plighted word, he dared not carry a weapon. His fingers would be too practiced in the art of whipping it forth, and in time of need they would act without his volition. The gun would suddenly appear in his hand and would be discharged before conscience and memory could stop him. Indeed, all the perils that he had previously faced in his life would be nothing compared with the troubles to which the good old woman had consigned him with the promise that she had exacted.

And so, going thoughtfully, and down-headed, along the hall, quite heedless now of the noise that his footsteps made—that being the difference between guilt and an innocent mind—he was quite unaware of a door swinging softly ajar behind him. It was not until he heard the voice, raised barely above a whisper, that he turned.

It was Mary Thomas, a figure to be guessed at rather than seen. Behind her, the shaded lamp, further obscured by the back of a chair pushed up against it, sent a broad film of light straight up toward the ceiling. But the radiance did not reach to her. It was rather the background against which she stood out.

The first thing he noted was the white gesture of her hand waving him toward her. The second thing he saw was that she had not prepared to retire. And that item might mean anything. It might be explained, perhaps, by the curious manner in which she had watched him all through the earlier part of the evening. He went to her at once, for there was no graceful escape.

"I knew it would be this way," she said, as soon as he was close enough. "But you mustn't do it. Come in here a moment."

He obeyed without a word. She closed the door behind him and turned the key in the lock. And now, as she faced him, there was light enough to show her eyes dancing with excitement.

"You were going to leave?" she said at once. "You were going to leave forever?"

He hesitated. How much did she know?

"I think I understand," she said. "It was either one of two ways. You made a bet that you could do this cruel thing. Or else you were simply hungry and decided to do a bit of acting for the sake of a Christmas dinner."

He rubbed his big, bony knuckles across his chin and smiled at her rather foolishly.

"When did you find out?" he asked.

She did not understand. "It was perfectly clear to anyone with an eye to see. It was perfectly clear the moment you refused to open the packages that they gave you for Christmas. You wouldn't open them simply because they didn't belong to you."

"Hmm," muttered the wanderer. "If I'd thought about it, I would have opened 'em."

She shook her head, still smiling, still keeping

back something whose suppression excited her.

"You've been listening for me to start out?"

"I heard you when you left your room before. But I was too late to stop you. I was afraid then that you had gone for good. But I peeked into your room and saw your coat, so I was sure that you had simply gone out for walk. I wanted to talk to you, you see? That's why I've been waiting and watching, and all the time the idea has been growing."

"Fire it at me," Happy Jack said. "I'm tolerable open to good ideas all the time."

"It's simply this, that if you go away now, you'll break Missus Neilan's heart. I know her. She isn't very well, and she isn't very strong. Such a shock as this would be about the end, I think."

"I don't quite follow the drift," said Happy Jack. "You know I ain't Johnny, and yet you seem to be figuring that I had ought to stay here?"

"Why not?" she said with a wide gesture. "Why not? Don't you like the place?"

"But what's that got to do with it? It ain't mine, lady."

"It has everything to do with it. You can have it if you want it."

He gaped at her.

"How far away is your own country, the place where people know you?"

84

"Oh, around about five days' stiff riding, I guess."

She clapped her hands, triumphant. "Then it's settled. You'll stay."

"Miss Thomas," he said soberly, "this sure is queer talk."

"It's right talk and true talk. No matter what made you come here, Providence was behind it. It was intended for the best. This is the place you belong. Johnny is dead. Everyone really knows that . . . everyone except the old folks. And they'll never believe. So let them have their belief, because they'd die without it. Let them have it and think that you are he."

"Do you think I'm lowdown enough to do a thing like that?"

"No. I think you're big and fine enough to do it. Oh, I know you're honest, and that it goes against the grain to think of such a thing as that which I suggest. But at bottom, isn't it a bit of charity?"

"Things that are built upon lies, lady, don't usually last particular long, from what I've seen. Some folks may call it charity, and some folks may call it another thing . . . but a lie is pretty apt to be a lie, and that's an end to it."

He shook his head with such finality that the argument seemed ended on the spot. And still she persisted.

"The ranch has been like a graveyard. There has never been a smile or a laugh, so far as I

85

can remember, until tonight. There has been no kindness, no thought for others, until you came. Oh, this evening it seemed to me that you were working a miracle. And that's why I'm asking you to stay."

"And you ain't joking?"

"Joking? I tell you in all seriousness that I really think it's a matter of life or death to them. Mister Neilan has had no interest in life for years, and Missus Neilan has simply been living in the hope that Johnny would come back. And if you disappoint her, I know the effect. It will be murder, just as certainly as though you pressed a revolver against her temple and fired!"

He wavered. "Is it square?" he said. "Is it square to even think about playing a trick like that?"

"Not for some people. But for you, yes. Because you're honest."

"Are you sure of that?" he asked.

"Hasn't every word you've said to me gone to prove it?"

She had stepped close to him while she spoke, and now she made a gesture of such lasting trust in him, and smiled up at him so perilously near, that the sense of her went to the brain of Happy Jack and made his heart leap.

"I'm going to show you how much I'm worth a trust like that," he said at length. "Will you come with me for a minute?"

He led the way to his own room. He opened the door. He pointed to the telltale pile of money on top of the bureau with the long revolver weighing it down.

She went close to examine it, made sure of what it was, and then started back with a soft exclamation of dismay. And the frightened eyes that she turned on Happy Jack hurt the big man more than a blow.

"You see how it is, and you see how much I can be trusted," he said.

"That's what you came for?"

"Yep. That's what I came for."

"Someone else put it into your mind. You never thought of it by yourself."

"How come you figure that?"

"Why, simply because you couldn't go through with it. You did all the hard part of the work, and then, when you had merely to walk out of the house with the money, you stopped and left it there. Why, if I thought you were honest and to be trusted before, I know it now."

Happy Jack shook his head. Such reasoning as this was beyond him.

"Besides," she was saying suddenly, "it isn't only for the sake of the old folks. I'm partly selfish about it. I've dreaded every vacation, because every vacation brought me back to the ranch. But if there were . . . were a human being here who knew how to smile . . . why, it would be wonderful to come back to the mountains, because I love them."

Happy Jack caught his breath. Her color had mounted as she spoke. And, though she could never be really beautiful, she was so pretty at that moment, so clear of eye, so wonderfully fresh in her young womanhood, that Happy Jack believed until that moment he had never known a woman worth looking at.

"I got few rules to live by," he said after a moment of staring at her, "but one of 'em is never to refuse a girl what she asks for. And if you really mean what you say . . ."

"I'll shake on it," broke in Mary Thomas.

He took her hand and pressed it gently.

IX

The bedroom of Mr. and Mrs. Neilan was on the first floor of the house with a big window opening onto the verandah, and the wife had barely finished detailing to her smiling husband the account of her interview with the wanderer, when a light tapping came against that window.

"How come anybody to be rapping at the window?" growled John Neilan. "And at this time of night!"

"It's only the wind shaking the pane," said his

wife. "There can't be anyone out there in the storm."

"Hark at that! There is someone."

It was unmistakable this time—three strong taps, equally spaced—and John Neilan, slipping out of bed into a capacious bathrobe, tucked his old feet into slippers and picked up the Colt that he always kept at hand near his bedside.

"John," cautioned Mrs. Neilan, "you aren't going to answer that knock with a gun in your hand?"

"Why not?"

"It's Christmas Day! That's why. No good will come of it. I know. Surely this day of all days is for gentleness."

"Gentleness . . . stuff!" grunted Neilan.

He went to the window and cast it up suddenly, at the same time stepping to one side in case some enemy attempted a direct attack by leaping into the room. But there appeared at the window the gray head of Chip Flinders, the oldest of their cowpunchers. He was obviously in a state of the most intense alarm, his jaw set hard and his eyes glancing hastily from side to side.

"What fool business is this?" Neilan grumbled.

"I didn't dare come around the front way," said Chip Flinders, his voice husky with fear. "He might've seen me."

"Who might have seen you?"

"Him," and he pointed above his head.

The rancher regarded Chip a moment from beneath the shadow of scowling brows. "Come in," he growled at length.

And Chip stepped through the window and stood turning his hat uneasily in his hands and looking from side to side at the carpet, so as to avoid looking at Mrs. Neilan, who was sitting bolt erect in the bed, hugging a cloak around her shoulders.

"Now," said the rancher, "talk straight and talk quick. You ain't the kind to come around packing fool yarns to me, Chip. What's got into your head tonight?"

"I figured I knew him the minute I clapped eyes on him," said the cowpuncher hurriedly, "but I couldn't place him, and I began figuring hard. But the harder I figured, the farther away I stayed from getting at him. I was plumb in bed and lying there almost asleep when it popped into my head. I seen the whole thing over again, and I knew him."

"Knew who, idiot? Who are you talking about?"

"Him that calls himself your son. And he's no more your son than I am."

There was a faint cry of alarm from the bed.

"It isn't true," Mrs. Neilan moaned. "I tell you, John, I'd swear it's Johnny. He . . . he's promised never again to use a gun just because I asked him. Isn't that proof?"

Chip Flinders suddenly began to laugh. "Excuse me, ma'am," he said. "You mean to say Happy Jack said he wouldn't pull a gun again in a fight? Why, lady, he could just about as soon stop drawing his breath as stop drawing his gun. His Colt is his third hand. It's his brains. Down south, they say he does his thinking with it."

"Happy Jack?" Neilan said. "You call him Happy Jack?"

"Don't listen to him, John," pleaded the wife. "Ah, I knew this would bring bad luck! But don't talk to him any longer!"

"Hush up," growled Neilan. "I'm going to get at the truth of this. Maybe Johnny went by the name of Happy Jack down south. What of it?"

Chip Flinders shook his head.

"Tell your story. Take your time," Neilan insisted. "I'll wait and listen patient till you're all through. This is tolerable important, Chip. If you're wrong, you're done with me. If you're right, I'll see that you don't lose none by opening my eyes to an impostor. Now take a breath and get your brain to working and start in."

Chip Flinders obeyed these instructions to the letter, bowed his head a moment in thought, and then looked up.

"You remember when I got restive about five years back?" he said.

"The time you quit and went south to do some prospecting?"

91

"Sure. That's the time."

"It was a fool thing to do. You came back broke . . . nothing left of all your savings."

"Right enough. I come back broke, but I sure got my money's worth in experiences."

"When a gent's got gray hair, it's time for him to let somebody else do the collecting of experiences."

"Maybe. But this experience that I had is sure something you can be glad of, Mister Neilan."

"Huh," grunted the rancher. "Go ahead, and I'll see."

"It was down in the town of Lesterville," began Chip Flinders. "I'd made a little stake up working a vein that pinched out on me just when I thought I'd struck it sure enough rich. I come down into Lesterville and put eight hundred in the bank, which was a tidy little stake and would see me get all fixed and started for another flyer at the mountains and the mines. Left me about three hundred dollars, and I started out to liquor up and have a large time, generally and all around.

"Which I was doing pretty good in a small way when there was a bunch of shooting started in town, and a lot of folks begun to rear and tear around. And pretty soon we got word that Bill Tucker's gang had just passed through, stuck up the cashier in the bank, and cleaned out the safes with a dust cloth. He didn't leave a penny behind him.

"I ain't a fighting man, but when I heard that and figured all was gone up in smoke, it sure hit me hard. I run out and tossed a saddle on my bronc and tore around and got to the center of town in time to join in with the posse that was starting. Sheriff Brown was running the party. I guess you've heard about Brown even away up here . . . but down there he still is pretty much looked up to. He'd a pile rather fight than eat. I seen him sitting his horse and giving directions about how some of the boys should start in one direction and some should start in another. But every now and then he'd stop and turn around and ask a question of a gent that was sitting a horse beside him, like he wanted to have that gent check up on what he was doing and say it was all right.

"It seemed to me pretty queer that a man like Brown would have to ask advice of anybody, even a judge, so I took a good look at the stranger. And they was a lot to see. He was only a kid, not much more than twenty, I guess. But he was sure built for keeps. Big wide shoulders and a thick chest, and always grinning and laughing and treating this like it was the beginning of a fine party. I turned to a gent nearby me, and I asked him who that was.

" 'You don't know him?' he says, turning around and looking at me sort of queer.

" 'No' says I. 'I sure don't. Who is he?'

" 'Before this here party is over you'll find out,' he says. 'That's Happy Jack, and you can lay to it that the trail he makes Tucker run will be the hottest that skunk ever traveled over. And that's the straight of it. That's Happy Jack. A plumb nacheral fighting man, son. The kind you heard your dad talking about that used to frolic around in the days of 'Forty-Nine. Well, Happy Jack is a ringer for that kind. He makes a gun talk Spanish when he feels like it.'

" 'Regular killer?' says I.

" 'Nope. Fighter. Not killer. He don't fight to get notches on his gun.'

"Well, after that I sure watched Happy Jack close. When the sheriff was ready to start, he took most of us boys with him, but Happy Jack picked out half a dozen gents and rode off another way.

"I asked where he was going, and somebody told me that he was going to try to head off Tucker by a short cut across the mountains. But the gent that told me said they wasn't no chance of him doing it, that short cut being plain murder on a horse.

"Anyway, Happy Jack started off and disappeared, and the rest of us buckled down and started to follow Sheriff Brown. We headed straight up a valley out of Lesterville. We rode hard, too, I'll tell a man. They was fifty-two gents started that trail, by my way of counting. When he got up the valley, they was only eighteen left.

I had that Molly pinto, and that was the only reason I was left in the running. Sheriff Brown sure used up horseflesh when he hit a trail.

"And it done him some good, too, for pretty soon, away off in the moonlight, when we rounded a hill, we seen Tucker's men scooting away. When they seen us, they let out a yell that we could hear, the whole bunch of 'em, and they lit out as hard as they could ride. They was weighted down by a lot of gold. But our horses were all plumb fagged by the hard work they'd done already. First we lost ground, and then we picked it up. On the open we could run faster than Tucker's men, but when it come to climbing, they sure had us beat.

"Looked like we could go on forever and never get no closer to 'em. And our horses was beginning to roar, they were so plumb tired. We was all about to give up the fight, when all at once a shooting started right ahead of us up the valley, and Sheriff Brown, he lets out a yell.

" 'It's Happy Jack!' he hollers. 'It's Happy Jack, boys, and he's sure made the short cut. He must've turned his men and horses into goats to get up there.'

"But there wasn't no doubt about it. Pretty soon, down come the Tucker gang . . . eleven instead of the fourteen we'd first counted, and we knew that Happy Jack had counted for three of 'em.

95

"Tucker tried to rush us. But eleven ag'in' eighteen wasn't no easy chance for him. We give him some quick fire. We emptied a couple of saddles and, when they turned to run up the valley again . . . there being no manner of ways for them to climb the sides of that ravine . . . we give it to 'em again, and even in the moonlight we shot good enough to drop another of 'em.

"You can count for yourself. That left eight gents ready to fight for their lives, and all heading up the valley straight for Happy Jack. They was bad ones, that gang of Tucker's. Nothing they wouldn't do. They'd burned and murdered and tortured and robbed. A choice lot of devils they was, every one. And now they had to fight for their lives.

" 'How many men did Happy get through the mountains by the short cut?' hollers the sheriff. 'How many? But Lord help 'em if they can't turn Tucker back before he gets to close quarters. Ride, boys! Ride!'

"And thinking about Happy and the rest of the boys . . . which couldn't't've been more'n two or three that he'd got through the short cut . . . we sure did punish our horseflesh to get up in time to help.

"But, when experts are fighting, it don't take long to end a scrap. We heard a crackling and a booming and a smashing of guns up the valley. And then came a couple of yells that made your heart stop beating. And then all at once there was a dead silence. There wasn't even a whisper. Just that cold, white moonshine a-pouring down on the valley.

" 'They've busted through!' called out Brown. 'Lord help Happy and the rest. Tucker must've busted through!'

"Up the valley we go like a shot. Pretty soon we get near the place. We see one of Tucker's men lying on his back with his arms throwed out. Then we come on three strung out one after another. And we knew that they'd dropped while they was rushing a big bunch of rocks right ahead of us. We galloped for them rocks. Right on the top of them we seen another of Tucker's men fallen on his face. And there was a second inside the rocks. That made six we found dead or wounded bad.

"What we seen next was sure a funny picture. It was Happy Jack sitting there in the moonshine with his back against a rock smoking a cigarette, with two dead men at his feet. We come to him with a yell.

" 'Are you hurt bad?' asked Brown, putting his arms around Happy like Happy was his own kid.

" 'They drilled me,' Happy says, quiet as you please. 'But I think that I'll pull through, right enough. Mind that poor devil there, though, will you? I think he's got a spark of life in him. He needs help more'n me.'

"We turned that gent over. It was Tucker. And he was just kicking out.

" 'Carry me over to Jack,' he says.

"We done it. It sure rides hard not to do what a dying man asks, even when he's a murdering skunk like Tucker was. We carried him over, and he puts out his hand to Happy.

" 'If I'd had you with me, kid,' he says, 'I'd've beat the world. So long, and good luck.'

"And then he died.

" 'But where's the rest of the boys, Happy?' says the sheriff, while we work like fury tying up Happy's wounds, and him never making a murmur.

" 'They didn't get here,' says Happy. 'The going was pretty rough.'

" 'You stood 'em off all alone?' says the sheriff.

" 'I had to,' says Happy and grins.

"And that was the honest truth. He'd done that fighting all by himself. And he'd won out. And that man, that Happy Jack, is the gent that's in your house tonight calling himself your son."

"And why not?" Mrs. Neilan asked, her voice trembling. "Surely we'd be proud to have such a hero for a son."

"Sure you would," Chip Flinders said, and nodded kindly. "But, you see, I asked about Happy Jack. He'd been brought up around Morgan Run, which was the name of the creek that run down the valley where he killed Tucker.

Somebody passing through left a baby behind 'em, and that baby was raised by everybody in general and nobody in particular, and because of his grin they got to calling him Happy Jack. They remembered him since he was a baby, and Johnny didn't leave home till he was fourteen, pretty near."

Mrs. Neilan dropped her face in her hands. Her husband rose and strode to and fro in the room.

"He looks like Johnny," he said. "But he sure ain't got Johnny's mean streak in him. And . . . Chip, heaven help you if you're lying to me."

"Do I look like I was lying?" Chip asked. "And do you think I'd talk ag'in' a gunfighter like Happy Jack if I didn't know that I was right? Ain't I taking my life in my hands by saying what I've said?"

"Them that bring bad-luck tidings don't get much thanks," said the rancher. "Almost I wish you hadn't told me. But what would Happy Jack be doing here?"

"He's trailed crooks and fought crooks and lived with crooks. And them that live free and easy are kind of apt to get free and easy. Ain't you got a pile of money in your safe down in the cellar?"

Neilan started. "Money? I should say! You think he come to make a play for that?"

"John, John!" Mrs. Neilan moaned. "Are you going to give him no chance to clear himself?

99

Even if I swear that I know he's good and honest, even if he ain't my boy?"

"And I gave him the key, like an idiot," groaned the rancher. "If the money's gone, I deserve losing it."

Gathering his revolver in a closer grip, he ran out of the room.

X

Down into the cellar ran Neilan, as fast as his old legs would carry him, and one glance at the open door of the safe was enough. He whirled and labored back up the stairs with teeth set and his gun poised. Not that he had any real hope of finding Happy Jack in the house, but he was in a fighting humor, and the touch of the rough gun butt was soothing against his palm.

He started straight for the room that Happy had slept in. But a whisper of voices in the hall, as he approached the top of the stairs, gave him pause.

Flat against the steps he dropped and, pushing the revolver ahead of him, he raised his head to look. He saw Happy Jack and the girl standing side by side. What they said he could not make out. But what happened he could easily see. In the hand of Happy Jack there was a thick wad of greenbacks, and he transferred the entire bundle of money to the hands of the girl. Then, with a wave of the hand, he turned away down the hall.

The master of the house waited to see no more. He whirled and scurried down the stairs as fast as he could run, blessing the age that had withered him to such lightness that his footfall made no sound on the boards.

He whisked into the safety of his room and confronted his wife and Chip.

"You're right, Chip," he said, "and I'm sure thanking you for what you told me. He done it. The safe's open, and the money's gone. And then I sneaked up to find him in his room, thinking he might not've gone yet. And he hadn't. He was still here. He was in the hall talking to the girl. And what do you think the fox has done?"

"Talking to Mary?" Mrs. Neilan gasped.

"Aye, he's bought her out. That's the gratitude she returns us for giving her a home. I seen him put the money in her hands. Don't you see how he figures? Suppose he's trailed and caught? He'll pass it off easy. He'll say that coming here was just a joke. He played the joke, and he left before morning. We say he busted open the safe and done burglary. He says . . . 'Then where's the money I took?' And there's no money on him! Why? Because he's left it with the girl. And afterward she's to slip away and send him the stuff, or half of it. She's always hated us. I've seen it in her quiet ways and the look she gives us now and then. And now she's going to have money enough to start her out in life."

He ground his teeth in his fury.

"We'll change that. We'll teach her, the vixen! And if being caught with stolen goods means the penitentiary in this state, I'm sure going to see that she lands there."

"John!" broke in his wife, wringing her hands. "Won't you listen to reason? Won't you please listen to me? There must be some explanation. If you'll only wait, you'll find out that neither Happy Jack nor Mary mean anything wrong."

"Are you plumb losing your mind?" exclaimed her irate husband. "Didn't I see the door of the safe open? Didn't I see him making her a Christmas present of the money? He's leaving the house right now."

He raised his hand to hush them. And in the breathless interval of silence, all three could hear the soft thud of a closing door. Neilan roused himself suddenly, and in the space of a few seconds he had thrust his legs into trousers, his feet into shoes that he did not pause to button, and huddled a coat over his thin shoulders.

"You're not going to follow him?" cried his wife. "Oh, John. I wish I'd never been born!"

"Hush up!" commanded her husband. "There he goes now."

Peering through the window, they saw the tall figure of Happy Jack striding through the starlight across the snow.

• • •

Happy Jack went slowly, realizing that he had gone out to face the second great danger that he had confronted tonight. But in the first event he had imperiled his honor and, now that this was safe, he looked forward to his meeting with Sandy Crisp as a lesser thing. Had he been able to bring his revolver with him, the adventure would have been an actual pleasure. But the promise to Mrs. Neilan bound him to helplessness in that respect.

Approaching the outskirts of the pines, he slackened his pace still further. Somewhere in that covert Crisp was waiting and perhaps Shorty Dugan was with him. The pines shut out the starlight and the haze of the westering moon after he had taken a few steps past the verge. He paused now, and whistled softly, raising his head so that the notes would travel as far as possible down the wind, which hummed and purred and whined through the upper branches.

After that he went on again, whistling a short note every few steps, until he came into a little clearing. He had hardly entered it when a hand fell without warning upon his shoulder and, staring about, he found himself face to face with Crisp, with Shorty grinning in the background.

"You got the stuff?" Sandy asked eagerly. And he rushed on, without waiting to hear an answer, as though he took success for granted: "But why didn't you go by the stable and get your horse?"

But the larger man shook his head. "I ain't got the stuff," he said simply.

"You didn't get the key?"

"No," lied Happy Jack.

But Sandy Crisp began to chuckle softly.

"That'd make a good Christmas story," he declared, "but I ain't no ways in the humor for hearing yarns. It's too cold, and we been waiting for you till we're all froze up. Don't lie, Happy. Do you think that we let all that party run along without watching? Not us! I slipped up and watched through the window. It was dead easy. And I seen with my own eyes when the old fool give you the key. So pony over the stuff, Happy, and we'll be on our way as soon as you can get your horse. I don't blame you for wanting to hog the whole lot of it. But I'm onto your game, Happy."

Still Happy shook his head.

"You want to know what happened, Sandy?" he said.

"Sure I do," said the other. "But what's that?"

"Where?"

"I heard somebody break through the snow . . . that sort of crunching sound, anyways."

"Maybe a branch fell. They ain't anybody out here. Nobody knows I left the house."

"Go look over there behind that brush, Shorty, and see."

Shorty obeyed, but his survey of the gloom behind the thicket was a most cursory one. He came back with the report: "All clear. Nobody there."

"All right," said Sandy. "Now go on with your yarn, Happy. And make it quick."

"I got the key," said Happy Jack, "and I went down from my room and opened the safe and took out the loot."

"That sounds like straight stuff." The outlaw grinned as he moistened his lips.

"And then," went on Happy, "old Missus Neilan came in and talked to me. She sure is a fine old lady, Sandy."

"So you give her back the money?" Sandy sneered. "Come straight, now, Happy. Maybe I know more'n you think."

"I didn't give her the money," Happy Jack said. "But, when she got through talking and left, I sure done a pile of thinking. And I saw that it was all a bum play, Sandy. I was playing the part of a sneaking coyote with folks that trusted me. You say that old Neilan is hard. Maybe he is, but he sure showed me a white hand all the way through. Anyway, I got to thinking, and finally I made up my mind that there wasn't enough money in this game to buy me off. I've lived straight, Sandy, up to now, and from now on I figure on going extra straight. I gave that money to the girl, Mary Thomas, to put back in the safe, because I wouldn't trust myself to handle that much coin. I might weaken at the last minute, thinking how many years' pay was in the roll."

"Just like a fairy story, you being the fairy prince," Crisp said, still sneering. "Go on. I'm trying to listen. But I sure got a limit to my patience, Happy. What you figure on doing now?"

"There's an old man and an old woman in that house, Sandy, that figure I'm their boy. Well, you know I ain't. But I've made up my mind that if I can give 'em any happiness by playing the part, I'm willing to try. I'm going back there and live like I belong in that family."

There was a moment of silence. The wind had dropped into a lull, and the hard breathing of Sandy Crisp was audible.

"Of all the lies I've ever heard," he said at last, "this is the father and the grandfather of the lot, and I've sure heard some fine liars working in their prime days. But, do you think I'm fool enough to believe you, Happy?"

Happy Jack shrugged his shoulders. "That ain't worrying me none."

"And you expect me to believe, too, that because your holster is empty, you ain't got a gun, maybe?"

"I promised Missus Neilan that I wouldn't carry a gun, Sandy, and I'm living up to the promise."

Sandy Crisp choked, and then broke into loud,

indignant laughter. "Am I dreaming, maybe?" he cried at length. "Am I having a funny dream? Pinch me, Shorty, so's I can wake up. Why, Happy, you fool, you're getting weak-minded. Don't you think I know you wouldn't come out and face me with that lie and without a gun?"

"I've told you straight," Happy Jack stated quietly.

"Then," said the outlaw savagely, "you might've shot yourself first and saved me the trouble."

"Wrong, Sandy. I know you're a hard one, but even you won't pull a gun on a gent that has bare hands."

"Won't I? You don't know me, Happy. Not by a long ways."

He swayed a little from side to side, very much as though the wind were unsteadying him, and yet at that moment there was not a breath. The dull moon haze fell softly into the clearing. The figures of the men stood out big and black and half obscured.

"I'm going to give you one more chance, Happy," said the outlaw. "Are you going to come across with that coin, or do you aim to start in pushing daisies?"

"I'm done talking," said Happy Jack, and turned on his heel.

He had almost reached the edge of the shadow when Sandy Crisp shouted: "Happy!"

Slowly he turned. The gun was already gleaming in the hand of Sandy, and the exclamation of Happy was drowned in the report that followed. Happy Jack slipped sidewise into the snow.

"Turn him over. See if he's dead!" exclaimed Sandy Crisp. "And then we'll make a break for . . ."

The last of his sentence was blotted out in a sudden fusillade from that same thicket that Shorty had been ordered to search the moment before. Shorty, with a yell of agony, leaped high in the air and landed running. In an instant he had disappeared among the farther trees. Sandy Crisp had doubled over at the sound of the first shot and fled with wolfish speed into the covert.

The uncertain light, and arms and hands numbed by the wait in the cold of the night, accounted for that poor shooting. John Neilan and Chip Flinders started out of their hiding place, cursing their erratic aim. Chip still was firing shot after shot through the trees beyond and shouting at the top of his lungs to the cowpunchers in the far-off bunkhouse. But, long before any response came, they heard the rapid crunching of the hoofs of galloping horses beating away through the snow.

In the meantime, John Neilan had dropped on his knees in the snow and with frantic efforts had turned the body of Happy Jack. He lay face up at length, a flow of crimson covering one side of his head. And suddenly his eyes opened and he stared about him.

"All right, Sandy," he muttered. "You'll get yours for this, you hound."

"It's not Sandy!" cried Neilan. "It's John Neilan! Chip! Chip! He's dead!"

The eyes had closed again.

But he was not dead. The scurrying crowd of half-dressed cowpunchers, coming in answer to those alarms of guns and shouts, lifted Happy Jack and carried him toward the house—carried him tenderly, in obedience to the frantic directions of John Neilan, freely interspersed with terrific curses directed at those who stumbled under the burden.

Halfway to the house they were met by a flying figure. It was Mary Thomas, and at her coming, John Neilan ran a pace or two to meet her and turned her back.

"It's all right," he kept saying. "There's nothing wrong. Just an accident. He's going to get well. He sure has got to get well."

And so they brought him eventually back into the ranch house and into Neilan's own bedroom, where his wife was cowering against the walls with her face sheltered behind her hands.

But when she saw what they had brought to her, she rose nobly to the occasion. Not even Mary

Thomas could share in the direction of what was to be done. With quick, quietly delivered orders, in five minutes she had every man busy with a different task, one kindling a fire, another running for bandages, a third washing the wound, and a fourth standing by in reserve.

Hardly a word other than orders was spoken until well on into the night. In fact the dawn of the Christmas Day was beginning to appear when the doctor, who had been summoned, arrived.

His examination was quickly ended.

"It's not fatal," he said. "The bullet traveled almost the whole length of the side of the skull. He may not waken for two hours more. That's all."

A faint cry from Mary Thomas made him turn.

"Is this his wife?" he said kindly, as she dropped on her knees beside the bed.

"You're speaking sort of previous, Doc," said John Neilan. "But I dunno how it'll turn out."

"How did it happen?" asked the doctor.

"That's a long story. The main thing is the ending. My boy is going to get well."

"John," whispered Mrs. Neilan, "what do you mean?"

"Why," John Neilan said, scratching his head, "ain't it all pretty clear. Why, you yourself said that there was Providence in it. And I guess there is. This is Christmas Day, ain't it? And ain't Happy Jack sure meant to be our gift? Besides, he's lacking a last name, and I figure that he'll take kindly to the name of Neilan."

"Heaven be praised," Mrs. Neilan whispered, "for making you see the light."

And as she spoke a red radiance fell across the room. The Christmas sun was rising through a clear, clear sky.

JERICO'S
GARRISON
FINISH

I

When Sue Hampton looked down to the pale, lithe hands that were folded in her lap, Jim Orchard had his first opportunity to examine her face. He thought her whiter than ever, and thinner, and he disliked the heavy shadows around her eyes. But when she looked up to him, the thick lashes lifting slowly, he forgot the pallor.

That slow trick with the eyes had first won him—that, and a certain wistfulness in her smile. There was nothing direct and commanding about Sue. Most girls a tithe as pretty as she were in the habit of demanding things. They accepted applause and admiration, as a barbarian king accepts tribute from the conquered. It was no more than their due. But it seemed to Jim that Sue Hampton was never quite sure of herself.

She turned her engagement ring absently and waited for Jim to go on.

"Let's see," he said, going back with difficulty to the thread of his story. "I left off where . . . ?"

"You and Chalmers had started for the claim."

"Sue, you don't seem half glad to see me."

He went to her, half angry and half impatient, and took her hands. They were limp under his touch, and the limpness baffled him. The absence of resistance in her was always the stone wall which stopped him. Sometimes he grew furious. Sometimes it made him feel like a brute.

"I am glad to see you," she said in her gentle voice.

"But . . . confound it . . . pardon me, Sue. Look up . . . smile, can't you?"

She obeyed to the letter, and he at once felt that he had struck a child. He went gloomily back to his chair. "All right," he said, "go ahead and talk."

"If you wish me to, Jim."

"Confound it, Sue, are you ever going to stop being so . . . so . . ."

"Well?"

"Oh, I don't know. Well, I'll tell you why I came back ahead of time."

"Ahead of time?"

"In a way. Someone drifted up where I was and told me that Garry Munn was hanging around and getting pretty thick with you."

There was no answer. That was one of the maddening things about her. She never went out of her way to show her innocence of blame, or to win over the hostile.

"Well . . . ," went on Jim Orchard, growing less and less sure of himself and more and more inclined to bully his way out of the scene, in spite of the fact that he loved her. "Well, Sue, is it straight? Has Garry Munn been around a lot?"

"Yes."

He had come some two hundred miles for the pleasure of seeing her, but chiefly for the joy of a denial of this tale.

"You mean to say that Garry is getting sort of ... sort of ... ?"

She did not help him out either by an indignant denial or laughter. Accordingly his sentence stumbled away to obscurity.

"Well," he said finally, "what do you think of him?"

"I like him a great deal."

He became seriously alarmed. "You don't mean to say that he's turned your head with his fine riding and all that?"

Tomorrow would be the last day of the great rodeo that had packed the little town of Martinville with visitors, and in that rodeo the spectacular name, from first to last, had been that of Garry Munn. In the bucking and roping and shooting contests he had carried away the first prize. The concern of Jim Orchard had some foundation. When he reached Martinville that day, the first thing of which he was told had been the exploits of Garry.

"Sue," he said suddenly, "what they told me is true."

She merely watched him in her unemotional way. In her gentleness there was a force that tied his hands. It had always been so. In another moment he was on his knees beside her chair, leaning close to her.

"Honey, have you stopped loving me?"

"No."

The beat of his heart returned to the normal. "Then say it."

"I love you, Jim." She turned on him those calm eyes that never winced, and which from the first had always looked straight into his heart.

"Just for a minute . . . ," he said, stammering, and then finished by touching her hands with his lips and returning to his chair. Another girl would have gloried in her triumph, but in the smile of Sue Hampton he saw no pride. How she did it he was never able to learn, but she was continually holding him at arm's length and wooing him toward her.

"I know you're the straightest of the straight," confessed Jim Orchard. "If you changed your mind about me, I'd be the first one to hear of it. Well . . . where was I?"

"You were telling me about the trip to the mines."

"Chalmers had the main idea. I staked the party, and we hit it rich!" He paused. The slight brightening of her face meant more to him than tears or laughter in another woman.

"I didn't want to see how things would pan out. The second day after we'd made the strike I asked Chalmers if he'd buy my share for five thousand. I didn't care much about having more than that. Five thousand was the figure you named, wasn't it? Five thousand before we could safely get married?"

"Yes."

"Chalmers jumped at the chance, and I beat it with the coin. Five thousand iron boys!"

"That was nearly five months ago?"

His jubilation departed. "You see, honey, on the way back I ran into McGuire. You know Mac?"

"I've heard you talk about him."

"Well, Mac was down and out. Doctor told him he'd have to take a long rest, and he needed a thousand to rest on. Lung trouble, you see? So, what could I do? There was a dying man, you might say, and I had five thousand in my wallet. What would you have done?"

"You gave him the money?" she countered, adroitly enough.

"I had to. And then, instead of going away for his rest, he blew it in one big drunk. Can you beat that, Sue?"

She was looking down at her hands again, and Jim began to show signs of distress.

"Well, I looked at my coin and saw that I was a thousand short. Four thousand was short of the mark, anyway, so I thought I might as well spend a little of it getting over my disappointment about Mac. I started out on a quiet little party. Well, when I woke up the next day, what do you think?"

"The money was gone, I think," said the girl.

"All except about a hundred," replied Jim. "But I took that hundred and started to play with it. I'm a pretty good hand at the cards, you know. For three months I played steadily, stopping when I'd won my percentage. The hundred grew like a weed. When I landed six thousand, I thought it was safe to quit. Just about then I met Ferguson. Fergie had a fine claim going. Just finished timbering the shaft and laying in a bunch of machinery. Mortgaged his soul to get the stuff sometime before, and they were pinching in on him. He needed four thousand to save forty. There wasn't any doubt that he was right. What could I do? What would you have done?"

"You gave him the money?" murmured Sue Hampton.

"I sure did. And then what do you think?"

"He lost it?"

"The mine burned, the shafts caved, and there was Ferguson flat busted, and my four thousand gone. But I took what I had left . . . and here I am with two thousand, Sue. I would have tried to get a bigger stake, and I would have made it, sure, but this news about Garry had me bothered a lot. I came back to find out how things stood and . . . Sue . . . I want you to take the chance. It's a small start, but with you to manage things we'll get on fine. Isn't two thousand enough in a pinch for a marriage?"

He had grown enthusiastic as he talked, but when she did not raise her eyes again the flush went out of his face.

"Jim, how old are you?"

"Thirty-two . . . thirty-three . . . never did know exactly which."

"Twelve years ago you had a whole ranch."

"Loaded to the head with debts."

"Not your debts. You came into the ranch without a cent against it. They were your brother's debts, and you took them over."

"What would you have done, Sue? Good heavens, there's such a thing as the family honor, you know. Billy didn't have any money, I did. What could I do? I had to make his word good, didn't I?"

"And the debts kept piling up until finally the ranch had to be sold."

"Ah," sighed Jim Orchard, remembering.

"For eight years you fought against it. Finally you were beaten. Then you became a manager for another rancher. You had a big salary and a part interest, but the rancher had a younger brother who couldn't fit into life. You stepped out and let the younger brother buy your interest for a song."

"What would you have done? It was his own brother. I couldn't very well break up a family, could I?"

"After that," went on the gentle voice, "you did

a number of things. Among others, you asked me to marry you. How long ago was that?"

"Three years ago last April Fifth."

She smiled at this instant accuracy—the small, wistful smile that always made the heart of Jim Orchard ache.

"And for three years we've been waiting to be married. Three years is a long time, Jim."

This brought him out of his chair. "Yes," he admitted huskily, "it's a long time."

"Don't stand there like . . . like a man about to be shot, Jim," she whispered.

He attempted to laugh. "Go on."

"I've kept on teaching school . . . and waiting."

"It's been hard, and you're a trump, Sue."

"But I think it's no use. You'll never have enough money. Not that I want money. But, if we marry, I want children . . . right away . . . and that means money."

"You know I'd slave for you and them."

"I know you would, and after you'd made a lot of money, somebody would come along who needed it more than we did."

"Never in the world, Sue!"

"You can't help it."

"You'd keep me from being a fool."

"I couldn't, because I believe in every gift you've ever made. What could I do?"

"Then . . . I'm simply a failure?"

"A glorious failure . . . yes."

"And that means?"

"That I'd better give back your ring."

"Is that final, Sue?"

"Yes."

"Then I was right. Mind you, I don't blame you a bit. I know you're tired out, waiting and hoping. And finally, you've stopped loving me."

She went to him with a smile that he was never to forget. "Don't you see," she said, "that every failure, which has made it a little more impossible for me to marry you, has made me love you a little more? But when we marry, we put our lives in trust for the children."

"And you couldn't trust me like that, of course."

"No." She held out the ring.

"Sue," he cried in agony, "when a man's sentenced to die, he isn't killed right away. Give me a chance . . . a time limit . . . a week . . . two days. I'll get that five thousand."

"If you wish it, Jim."

"First . . . put that ring back on."

"Yes."

He caught her in his arms in an anguish of love, of despair. "I'll get it somehow."

"But no violence, Jim?" All at once she clung to him. "Promise!"

In the past of Jim Orchard there had been certain scenes of violence never dwelt upon by his friends. There was a battered look about his face that time alone did not account for, or mere mental strain. In cold weather he limped a little with his right leg, and on his body there was a telltale story of scars.

Not that his worst enemies would accuse him of cruelty or malignancy, but when Jim was wronged a fiendish temper possessed him. Some of those tales of Jim Orchard in action with fist, knife, or gun came back to the girl, and now she pleaded with him.

"All right," he said at length. "I promise. It's two days, Sue?"

"Yes. One last thing . . . if any man . . ."

"All right. I've promised . . . and I won't harm him."

II

He went out and stood with his hat in his hand, heedless of the blinding sunshine. In the distance, from the field of the rodeo, there was a chorus of shouting, and Jim Orchard glared in that direction. In all the ups and downs of his life, this was the first time that the happiness of others had roused in him something akin to hatred.

They've given me a rotten deal. They've stacked the cards, thought Jim. And certainly he was right. The history of his hard work, all undone by fits of blind generosity which Susan Hampton had outlined to him, was only a small portion of the truth.

They said of Jim Orchard: "He's got a heart too big for his own good." And again: "An easy mark."

There was just a touch of contempt in these judgments. Generosity is a virtue admired nowhere more ardently than in the West, but reckless generosity never wins respect. Because of the speed of his hand and the accuracy of his eye, no one was apt to taunt Jim with his failings in this respect, but there was a good deal of talk behind his back. He knew it and despised the talkers.

But now his weakness had been driven home as never before. Jim felt that the world owed him something. He could be even more exact. He needed five thousand, and he had two thousand. In terms of cold cash he felt that the world owed him exactly three thousand dollars, and he was determined to get it. Sue had not judged him wrongly. For a moment, a grim determination to take by force what he needed had formed in his mind, but now his hands were tied, and that possibility was closed to him.

However, there were always the gaming tables, and his luck was proverbial. He turned in that direction to see a little procession coming slowly up the street. Four men were carrying another on a stretcher, and a small crowd was following them. They stopped near Jim Orchard to rest a moment.

"Jerico's got another man," he was told briefly.

He went to the side of the litter. It was Bud Castor, his face white with pain, the freckles standing out on his forehead. The heavy splints and bandages around his right leg and the swathing of his body were eloquent. Jerico had done a "brown" job of Bud. He had never seen the horse, but everyone had heard of Sam Jordan's great black stallion. As a rule he pitched off those who attempted to ride him. Again he might submit with scarcely a struggle, only to bide his time and attack his would-be master at an opportune moment with tigerish ferocity.

"Jim," pleaded the injured man, "do me a favor. Get your gat and plug that black devil, will you?"

But Jim Orchard turned and went on his way. After all, he felt a poetic justice in the deviltry of Jerico. They had run that black mustang for a whole season and, when they could not wear him down, had captured him by a trick. This was part of his revenge—a trick for a trick. Who could blame him?

Savagery of any kind was easily understandable by Jim Orchard on this day. In the meantime, he headed straight for the big gaming house of Fitzpatrick. He entered and walked straight to that last resort of the desperate—the roulette wheel. Fitzpatrick welcomed him with both a sigh and a smile; if he was a royal spender, he was also a lucky winner.

But the little buzz of pleasure and recognition that met Jim Orchard was not music to his ears today. He nodded to the greetings and took his place in the crowded semicircle before the wheel. He began playing tentatively, a five here, a ten there, losing steadily. And then, as all gamblers who play on sheer chance will do, he got his hunch and began betting in chunks of fifty and a hundred on the odd.

"Orchard has started a run," the rumor ran through the room, and the little crowd began to grow.

As he played, wholly intent on the work before him, he heard someone say: "Who'd he get?"

"Bud Castor. Nice for Bud, eh?"

"But who'll take care of Bud's family? Sam Jordan?"

"Bah! Sam Jordan wouldn't take care of a dog."

"They'll take up a collection, maybe."

"They's been too many collections at this here rodeo, I say, for one."

"And you're right, too."

Again the odd won, and Jim, raking in his money, prepared to switch his bets. His momentary withdrawal was taken advantage of by a squat-built, powerful fellow who touched his arm.

"How are you, Jim?"

"Hello, Harry. What you want?"

"How'd you know I was busted?"

"Are you flat, Harry?"

"I'll tell a man."

"What'll fix you up?"

"Sure hate to touch you, Jim, but if you can let a hundred go for a couple of days . . . ?"

"Sure."

His hand was on his wallet when he remembered—remembered about Sue Hampton, his grudge against the world, and that debt that he felt society owed him.

He hesitated. "Haven't you got a cent, Harry?"

"Not a red, partner."

Orchard set his jaw in the face of the ingratiating grin. From a corner of his eye he had noted the passing of a wink and a wise smile between a couple of bystanders. There followed a sudden scuffle, without warning, without words. At the end of it, Harry, with one arm crooked into the small of his back, had been jammed into the bar in a position of absolute helplessness, and the deft hands of Jim Orchard went swiftly through the pockets of his victim. Presently he found what he wanted. He drew forth the chamois bag, shook it, and a little shower of gold pieces fell to the floor.

He released Harry with a jerk that sent him spinning across the floor.

"A cold hundred if you got a cent," he declared.

"Is that what you call flat broke? You skunk!"

The crowd split away and drew back, like a wave receding from two high rocks. There was a very good possibility of gun play, and no one wanted to be within the direct course of the bullets. It required a very steady nerve to face Jim Orchard, but Harry Jarvis was by no means a coward. He was half turned away from Jim, with his face fully toward him, and the hidden arm was crooked and tensed, with the hand near the holster of his gun. The weight of a hair might turn the balance and substitute bullets for words. Jim Orchard was talking softly and coldly.

"You come to me like a drowned rat," he said, "and you beg for a hundred. Where's the hundred I gave you six months ago? There was another hundred before that, and a fifty and a couple of twenties still further back. You've used me like a sponge and squeezed me dry. And there's a lot of the rest of you that've done the same thing. Where's the gent in this room that's ever heard of me begging or borrowing a cent from anybody? Let him step out and say his little piece. But the next four-flushing hound dog that tries a bluff with me like Harry's is going to get paid in lead on the spot. Gents, I'm tired . . . I'm considerable tired of the way things have been going. There's going to be a change. I'm here to announce it."

Then he deliberately turned his back on Harry

Jarvis and stepped to the bar. Harry Jarvis, great though the temptation of that turned back was, knew perfectly well by the sternness of the faces around him that his gun would be better off in its leather than exposed to the air. Jarvis turned and disappeared through the door.

"Well, Jim," said the bartender, "there's a hundred saved."

"There's more than a hundred spent," answered Jim gloomily. "He's busted up my run."

For the gamester's superstition had a hold on Jim Orchard. Nothing could have persuaded him to tempt fortune again on that day, once his happy streak of winning had been interrupted from the outside. He counted his winnings as he left the gaming hall. He was some five hundred and fifty dollars ahead, as the result of the few moments he had spent in the place. At least it was a comfortable beginning toward the goal that had been set for him by Susan Hampton. When he reached the dust of the street, he had so far relaxed his grim humor that he was humming softly to himself. The result of his contentment was that he nearly ran over a barefooted urchin who was scuffing his way moodily through the dust.

"Hey!" yelled the youngster, "whatcha doing?" He changed to a surly grin. "Hello, Jim."

"Hello," said Jim Orchard. "You're Bud Castor's boy, I figure."

"Sure."

"What's the news? What's the doctor say?"

"He says Pa won't never be able to ride ag'in."

Fate made the fingers of Jim Orchard at that moment close over the money that he had just won at the gaming hall. Before the impulse left him he had counted out five hundred and fifty dollars into the hand of the youngster.

"You take that to your mother, you hear? Tell her to put it away for the rainy day. Or maybe she can use it to help get Bud fixed up."

"Gee," exclaimed the boy, "I . . . I'd about die for you, Jim Orchard!"

"Hmm," mused the spendthrift. "Now, you cotton on to this . . . if you ever tell your ma or your pa where you got the money, I'll come and skin you alive. Don't forget."

He accompanied this warning with a scowl so terrible that the child changed color. Jim Orchard left him agape and went on down the street, smiling faintly. When he reached the hotel, his smile went out suddenly.

"Good glory," said Jim, "I've done it again." But he instantly consoled himself in his usual manner. "What else was there for me to do? Bud needs it more than I do, I guess."

III

He was beginning to feel a certain leaden helplessness, as men will when they think that destiny is against them. He had had half of the five thousand in his pocket, but now he was back to the two thousand again. He went with a heavy step into the bar of the hotel and leaned against the wall. Here the heroes of that day's events at the rodeo were holding forth on their luck. With immense grins and crimson blushes they accepted the congratulations of the less daring or the less lucky. He was picked out by one or two and invited to drink, but he shook his head. The invitations were not pressed home, for Jim Orchard was obviously in one of his moods. At such times those who knew him best avoided him the most.

Only the hotel proprietor ventured to pause for an exchange of words. "How's things?"

"Rotten. I'd staked every cent I have on Jerico, and now he's out of the running for the race tomorrow."

"How come?"

"Ain't Bud Castor all mashed up? Who'll ride Jerico?"

"That's right. I forgot. Maybe you'd try a fling at him, Jim?"

"I'm not that tired of living, partner."

"Then there's no hope unless Garry Munn takes on the job."

Jim Orchard pricked his ears. "Yep, there's Garry. Handy on a horse, too."

"Not the man you are in the saddle," said the flattering host.

"I'm past my day," said Jim Orchard. "I've seen the time . . . but let that go. By the way, where's Garry?"

"Gone up to his room."

"I want to see him," replied Jim.

Having learned the room number, he straightway climbed the stairs.

What were the emotions that made it so necessary to see Garry Munn, he did not know until he had entered the room and shaken hands with the man. Then he understood. A strong premonition told him that this was the man who would eventually marry Susan Hampton. Here, again, there was a feeling of fate. Indeed, Garry Munn had so often secured the things he wished that it was hard to imagine him failing with the woman he wanted to make his wife. He was a fine, handsome fellow with a clear-blue eye and decidedly blond hair—the Scandinavian type. He was as tall as Jim Orchard, and far more heavily set. Altogether he was a fine physical specimen, and his brain did not lag behind his body. He had been born with the proverbial silver spoon in his mouth, and it was well known that he had improved his opportunities from the first. The ranch, which his father left him as a prosperous property, had been flourishing ever since, as Munn bought adjacent land. He was well on his way, indeed, to becoming a true cattle king. No wonder that Jim Orchard had to swallow a lump of envy that rose in his throat as he looked at his companion.

"I hear you been tearing things up at the rodeo," he began, "and walking off with the prizes, Garry."

"Because you weren't around to give me a run for my money," answered the diplomatic Garry. "How's things, Jim? How's mining coming on?"

"Rotten."

For all of his diplomacy, Garry could not keep a little twinkle of gratification out of his eye, and Jim felt an overwhelming desire to drive his bony fist into the smirk on the other's lips. He wanted trouble, and only his promise to Sue Hampton kept him from plunging into a fight on the spur of the moment.

"Mining's always a hard gamble," went on Garry.

"But the luck still stays good with you, Garry?"

"Tolerable."

"Sue has been telling me a lot about you."

"Oh." The diplomatic Garry became instantly wary.

"You been seeing a good deal of her lately, I guess?"

"Sure," said Garry Munn. "I tried to keep her company while you were out of town. No harm done, I guess?"

"Sure not. Mighty thoughtful of you, Garry."

Down in his heart he had always felt that Garry was a good deal of a clever sneak, and now he gave his voice a proper edge of irony. Yet the younger man was continually surprising him by unexpected bursts of frankness. One of these bursts came now.

"You see, Jim," he declared, "I always aim to let Sue know that, while I ain't running any competition with you, I'd rather be second best with her than first with any other girl around these parts."

"That's kind of consoling for Sue, I figure."

"Oh, she don't take me no ways serious. I'm just a sort of handy man for her. I take her around to the parties when you ain't here to do it. She treats me like an old shoe. Nothing showy, but sort of comfortable to have around." He chuckled at his statement of the case.

"Sort of queer," murmured Jim Orchard. "Here you are with mostly everything that I lack and still I got something, it appears, that you want for yourself."

"You don't mean that serious, Jim?"

"Mean what?"

"You don't think I'm trying to cut in between you and Sue Hampton?"

"Garry, all I think would near fill a book."

It was plain that Garry Munn did not desire trouble. He even cast one of those wandering glances around the room that proclaim the man who knows he is cornered. Then he looked steadily at his guest.

"Let's hear a couple of chapters."

"You been running a pretty good man-sized bluff, Garry. You been playing rough and ready all your life. Underneath I figure you for a fox."

"Kind of looks as though you're aiming at trouble, Jim."

"Take it any way you want."

Garry shrugged his shoulders. He saw the twin devils gleaming in the eyes of Orchard and knew what they meant. He had seen Orchard at work in more than one brawl, and the memories were not pleasant.

"You can't insult me, Jim."

"Seems that way," returned Jim Orchard. "Somehow, I never had a hunch that you was as low as this, Garry."

"What have I got to gain by fighting you up here? You're a shifter, a wastrel . . . pretty close to a tramp. Why should I risk myself in a mix-up with you? Where's the audience?"

"I'll try you in a crowd, Garry."

The other became deadly serious. "Don't do it,

Jim. Between you and me, I know you're a bad man in a fight. So am I. But in private I'm going to dodge trouble. If you cut loose in public, I'll fight back, and it'll be the hottest fight of your life."

"I think it would be," admitted Jim with candid interest, as he ran his glance over the powerful body of the other.

"Now that we've got down to facts," ran on Munn, "I don't mind saying that I'm out for you, Orchard. I'm out to get Sue Hampton, and I'm going to get her. In the first place she's waited long enough for you. In the second place there never was a time when you been worthy of looking twice at her."

"You get more and more interesting," said Orchard, smiling. He appeared to grow cooler as the other increased in heat. "But you never took no notice of Sue until I began to call on her."

"A good reason, Orchard. We started out with an even break. We both had ranches, and about the same layout of stock, and things like that. I made up my mind I was going to beat you out . . . and I did it. Who started by lending you money? I did. Who kept on lending? I did. And who finally bought the whole shebang? I did. I got your ranch, I got your cows, I got your horses. I put you right off the cow map."

"And you decided to keep right on?" queried Jim Orchard pleasantly.

"Why not? I started you downhill and I'm going

to keep you going. And the job ain't complete if I don't get your girl away from you. I'm going to get her. You can lay to that."

Orchard's face flushed crimson, as his hand instinctively reached out. Then he remembered his promise. With difficulty he controlled himself and moved toward the door. There he paused and looked back over his shoulder.

"It does me a pile of good to have the mask off your good-looking face, Garry. I've had one look at the skunk you are inside and I won't forget."

"Fair means or foul," Garry replied calmly, settling back into his chair. "I was always out for your scalp, Orchard, and now I'm sure I'm going to get it."

There was a tensing of the gaunt figure at the door, and for a moment Garry thought he had gone too far. But instead of making the fatal move toward his gun, Jim Orchard allowed his long face to wrinkle into a smile. He swept his hat in mock politeness toward the floor and then disappeared with his usual slow, stalking walk.

IV

Among the unnamed good things which Sue Hampton had done in her life, a prevented homicide was now to be numbered, and Jim Orchard was well aware of it as he closed the door and went down the groaning stairs. His muscles were still hard set, and he was struggling to keep himself in hand. When he reached the verandah, he stopped to breathe deeply, waiting for the red mist to clear away. But in spite of the passing of moments, the tips of the fingers of his right hand still itched for the feel of the handle of his revolver.

Into his mind cut the sharp, small voice of Sam Jordan. He turned and saw the man coming with difficulty toward him. His legs trailed behind him or wobbled awkwardly to the sides, as he dragged himself on with the crutches. For many a month, now, every waking moment of Sam Jordan's life had been a torture. His face was old and gray with pain, and his smile was a ghastly caricature. Yet he never complained; he never surrendered to whining.

He had been a sound and hale man when he attempted to ride Jerico. The former owner of that fierce mustang had a standing offer of the gift of the beast and five hundred dollars besides, to any man who could stay on his back for five minutes. Sam Jordan had made the attempt—and he stayed on for the prescribed length of time.

Sam's riding of Jerico was something of which even strong men still talked with a shudder. For Jerico had been posed by his captor as an "outlaw" and had already gone to a finishing school of bucking. There have been fables of men who could ride anything "on four feet and with hair on its back," but these are truly fables. Jerico was a king among outlaws. He leaped like a bouncing spring, and with equal uncertainty of direction, and his endurance was a bottomless pit.

He was full of freaky humors, however. Sometimes he pitched like a fiend, while on other occasions he demonstrated for only a moment or so and waited for another day, when he was more in the humor of deviltry. With Sam Jordan he began mildly with straight bucking as he ran. Then he turned and came back fence rowing, and then, getting warmed to his work, he commenced to weave. And still Sam Jordan stayed to his work, until, at the end of the fourth minute, the great black stallion began to sunfish.

Of all forms of bucking this is the most dreaded, and Jerico "fished for the sun" almost literally. In other words, he leaped a prodigious height and then came down on stiffened forelegs. The result was a shock that stunned the brain and nearly wrenched the head from the shoulders of Sam Jordan.

With only one minute remaining for him to fulfill his contract, Jordan was doing well enough when Jerico began his master work. The third of these grim shocks sent the blood bursting from the nose and mouth of the unfortunate Jordan. But Jerico was only beginning. He added a consummate touch. Instead of landing on both stiff forelegs, he struck on only one. The result was a heavy impact, and then a swift lurch to one side—a snap-the-whip effect. With glazing eye and awful face Sam Jordan stayed in the saddle, rapidly being jarred into unconsciousness.

But the minute slipped past, and exactly at the end of the scheduled five minutes, Jerico reared and pitched back. His whole weight crushed upon the body of Sam Jordan and, when the latter was raised from the ground, he was an unspeakable wreck with hardly six inches of sound bone in either of his legs. He was now the proud possessor of the fiend who had wrecked his body and his life.

One might have expected Sam Jordan to spend the rest of his days tormenting the wild mustang. He did quite the reverse. He managed to secure an old Negro named Tom who was the first and only human being the stallion could endure around him, and he made Tom care for the mustang as if for a great race horse. Nothing was too good for Jerico, as far as the fortune of Sam Jordan extended.

One by one Sam hired or tempted famous riders to back his horse. The results were usually disastrous. Sometimes it was merely a broken arm or leg; sometimes it was much worse. Sometimes, to be sure, a lucky fellow got off with merely a stunning fall. But the great danger from Jerico lay not in the fall, but in what was apt to happen afterward—for Jerico would whirl on the fallen man like a tiger and do his best with teeth and hoofs to end his life. Sooner or later, of course, he would succeed and kill his rider—and then it would be necessary to kill Jerico. In fact, why Sam Jordan allowed the beast to live was more than anyone could tell. Yet he professed a great affection for Jerico, and the mustang continued to live on the fat of the land.

Of late, an ugly rumor had sprung up to the effect that Sam Jordan, crippled for life and in constant torment, had come to hate the world, and he kept Jerico merely for the pleasure of seeing the great horse do to others as he had already done to Sam Jordan. But the whisper was so ugly that it was not generally believed. Indeed, it seemed that Bud Castor, the last hero to attempt the subjugation of Jerico, had almost succeeded. The horse had even begun to evince signs of affection for his rider and had never been known to buck his hardest when Bud was in the saddle. Today, however, had ended the reign of Bud Castor in a horrible manner. Jerico was once more free, and the thought of entering him in the race, which was to end the festivities of the rodeo, had become a complete illusion and a dream.

Something of all this went through the mind of Jim Orchard, as he watched Sam drag his body across the verandah. He picked up a chair and met the cripple halfway with it and forced him to sit down. Sam accepted it with a grunt. Lowering himself cautiously into it, he remained speechless for a moment, leaning on his crutches, with his eyes closed and his face covered with perspiration. The agony of moving that deformed body on the crutches would have brought groans from the most stoical, but after a while Sam recovered his self-possession and actually looked up to Jim with a smile. They were unpleasant things to see, those smiles of Jordan's. Still he did not speak until his breathing became regular and easy, and Jim Orchard, looking down at the other in horror and pity, did not offer to begin the talk.

"So you're back, Jim?" began the cripple.

"You see me. Back from the mines, Sam."

"And what luck?"

"My usual luck."

"That's been pretty bad, lately. Eh?"

"Worst in the world."

"Hmm."

Jordan changed the conversation suddenly. "Did you ever see Jerico run?"

"Never."

"Don't know how fast he is?"

"Sure. I have an idea. I've heard them tell how they ran him for a whole season with relays of fresh horses and never could get nearer than the

143

smell of his dust. He used to just loaf along and play with the fastest horseflesh they could bring out."

"Play with 'em . . . that's it." Sam chuckled. "He's a playful horse, is Jerico . . . playful all the way through, he is."

The thought convulsed him with silent mirth, which he checked to look slyly up at Jim Orchard, as though in fear the other might have understood too much. It was sickening to the cowpuncher.

He had known Sam in the old days, free and easy, good-looking, strong, recklessly brave, open of heart as a child. But now there was an indescribable malice in that face. He did not talk, but he purred with caressing tones, and under the purr Orchard was horribly conscious of the malignant heart. The fellow had suffered so much and so long that he seemed to be living on hatred.

"Fast," went on Sam. "Why, you ain't got no idea how fast he is. Why, Jerico could run a circle around the fastest horse that's entered for the race tomorrow. That's how fast he is. Sort of a shame he ain't going to have the chance at it, eh?"

"Too bad. No way of getting him ridden?"

"Not a chance, unless you'd try, Jim. That'd be a thing to see . . . a man that's never been throwed, and a horse that's never been rode! That'd be a thing to see."

All at once Orchard saw the whole point to the talk. Sam Jordan was up to his old tricks, and this time he had picked on Orchard to be the victim of this trained devil in the hide of a horse.

"Who told you I'd never been thrown?" demanded Jim. "I've been thrown, and often, too."

"Not that nobody knows about," put in Jordan eagerly. "Not that anybody around here remembers. Just this morning I heard a couple of the boys talking. 'Who's the best rider around these parts?' they say. 'Hawkins,' says one. 'Lorrimer,' says another. 'Garry Munn,' says another. 'You're fools, all of you,' says the first gent. 'They ain't one of 'em that can touch Jim Orchard. Why he's never been throwed!' That's the way they talk about you around these parts, Jim, and if you was to ride Jerico, everybody'd believe it."

The malice of the man was patent, now. He kept smiling and nodding so that it would be unnecessary for him to meet the eye of Jim Orchard. But why should he hate such an old friend and companion? Simply because he, Sam Jordan, was a shapeless wreck, and Jim Orchard was as tall and straight and agile as ever.

"It's no good, Sam. I won't try Jerico. My pride isn't that kind. I don't pretend to be the best rider in the world. Maybe I'm not half as good as the fellows Jerico has pretty near killed in the past."

Sam Jordan sighed. "I thought maybe I'd find you kind of down in the pocket. I figured on paying quite a bit if you could ride Jerico in the race."

Temptation surged up in the mind of Jim Orchard, but he shook his head. The memory of Bud Castor came back upon his mind. "I'm not your man, Sam."

"It ain't so easy to pick up a hundred every day."

"I'll take my money the harder ways, then."

"Or two hundred, say. I'd like to see my horse entered, Jim."

"Not any hope of it, as far as I'm concerned."

The face of Sam Jordan went black and he bowed his head for a moment. "Five hundred," he whispered suddenly, and Jim winced as though he had been struck.

"What makes you so sure that I've got a price today?" he asked fiercely.

"I can tell it by the hungry look you got in your eye. How about it? Five hundred, Jim, payable the minute that horse finishes the race."

"No. No use in talking, Sam."

"You're a hard gent to do business with. Well, here's my rock-bottom offer . . . one thousand cold iron men for you, if you ride Jerico in the race, Orchard."

"It's a lot of money," said Jim, "but it's not as much as I need."

"Besides, you can bet. The minute they know that Jerico is in the race the odds will drop. They won't give you even money, but for every three bucks you bet you can win two."

He paused, for the face of Jim Orchard had become troubled, and he wisely allowed the temptation to work. It was the way the proposition came pat that appealed to the gambling instinct in Orchard. He had two thousand, then a thousand from Jordan would make three thousand, and the amount won would add two thousand, making up the total of five thousand that he needed. It was almost as if Jordan knew the amount of money in his pocket and the need he had for exactly three thousand more.

"Sam," he said, "I take you."

"Good boy! I knew I'd fetch you." He was rubbing his hands together in glee. "When do you want to try out Jerico?"

"Now's as good a time as any. Go down and have him taken out into the corral. Do I have to rope him and saddle him, or do you give me a flying start?"

"Give you every sort of a start. All you have to do is climb into the saddle, and off you go."

But Jim Orchard turned away with a sick smile. He had not the slightest of hopes, only his gambler's instinct had ruled him, and the crushed body of Bud Castor came back into his mind with a premonition of death.

But if he were crippled, who would be the donor of five hundred dollars to "give him a chance?" Or would he live a cripple with a mind poisoned like that of Sam Jordan? He did one of those foolish things that the oldest and strongest men are apt to do now and then in a pinch. He took out a little leather folder from his pocket, opened a picture of Sue Hampton, and touched it covertly with his lips.

V

There was no need to spread the tidings through the village with messengers. It was late afternoon by this time and, the events of the rodeo having been entirely completed and the crowd packed back into the town to wait for the crowning glory of the race of the next day, rumor took up the tale of what Jim intended to attempt.

Most people were incredulous, but not only did rumor say he was to attempt the riding, but that he would make the first experiment with Jerico on that very day. It was remembered that he had passed the broken body of Bud Castor earlier in the day. The romantic took up the story and embroidered it. Jim Orchard, being an old friend of Bud's, had sworn to him to ride the stallion into submission, or else die in the attempt. The conversation between Bud and Jim was even invented and elaborated.

All this took place within some thirty minutes. At the end of that time Sue Hampton came to the hotel asking for Jim Orchard. She was shown to his room.

"Shucks," said the disgusted public, "she'll keep Jim from going through with it."

"You don't know Jim," answered the fat proprietor of the hotel. "Nothing'll stop him."

Jim Orchard had just finished dressing. He knew that he was about to take the center of the stage in a public manner, and whether it ended tragically or happily, he wanted to fit the great occasion. A rap at his door interrupted him, and he opened it to Sue Hampton.

He was so astonished by her appearance that he retreated before her into the center of the room as though she had presented a loaded revolver to his head. She closed the door behind her without taking her resolute eyes from him, and then she followed him a little ways.

"What's the matter, Sue?" he kept repeating helplessly.

For he was completely at sea. How had the dim, quiet Sue Hampton he knew been transformed into this creature with eyes of fire and trembling lips and flaring color?

"You coward!" cried Sue Hampton. "You coward, Jim Orchard!"

Orchard stood agape. "What's wrong, Sue?"

"You promised me that you'd play square . . .

and now you're going to ride Jerico . . . and get killed like Bud . . . oh, is it fair, Jim?"

"Bud wasn't killed. He . . ."

"What happened to him was worse. I know. I talked to the doctor. Lucky for Bud that you gave him five hundred dollars!"

So that was known. Jim set his teeth. If he ever found that worthless boy, he would skin him alive and throw the skin away. On this day of all days to have such a thing brought to the ear of Sue.

She went running on in a storm of protest. "It isn't the money. You know it isn't. All that I want you to prove is that you can make it and keep it long enough. And now you're throwing yourself away . . . do you think I could ever raise my head again if anything happened? I want you to promise that you'll not try to ride Jerico."

He took her by the arm and led her to the window. "Look down there."

A crowd of a hundred or more persons had gathered, and more people were constantly arriving.

"They're getting ready to go along with me when I start for Jerico. That's why they're there. Everybody in town knows that I've told Sam Jordan I'm going to ride the brute. Do you think I can back down, now?"

"You value your pride more than you do me, Jim."

He lost a good deal of color at her reply, but

he answered gravely: "It's more than pride. It's a matter of honor."

All at once she had slipped into his arms, and her hands were locked behind his head.

"Dear Jim. Dear old Jim. Tell me you won't?"

It was another revelation to Jim. Something in him started toward her like iron toward a magnet.

"We won't wait for the money. We'll marry now . . . today . . . this minute. But promise me to give up Jerico! Oh, I've seen that horse fight!"

"No."

He managed to say the word after a bitter effort. And the girl slipped away and looked at him, bewildered.

"Is that the last word, Jim?"

With despair he saw her returning to her habitual placidity. The fire died away and left her more colorless than ever. Her eyes went down to her folded hands.

"It's a matter of honor, Sue."

At that she went toward the door, and Jim, sick at heart, tried to stop her. Something about her lowered head, however, warned him not to touch her. She went out, the door closed, and he heard her light, quick step fade away down the hall. It was to Jim as if she had stepped out of his life.

It was a long minute later that the growing murmur of the crowd below gave him the courage to put on his hat and go down. When he came onto the verandah, there was a murmur, and then followed an actual shout of greeting. He saw the weaving faces in a haze. Particularly, as he remembered later, there was the handsome face of Garry Munn at the outskirts of the crowd, and Garry was indubitably worried.

The crowd trailed out behind Jim, as he went down the street, like the tail streaming behind a comet. He came to the shack where Sam Jordan was staying until the rodeo ended. Sam himself was seated in a wheelchair in front of the door, and he began waving and nodding a greeting to the crowd. He seemed in amazing good humor. But Jim Orchard had only a casual glance for the owner. His attention was for the horse. The great black stood in the corral where he had been roped, thrown, blindfolded, and saddled. He was still blindfolded, but as one who senses danger, he stood with his head thrown high and his ears flat against his neck.

Orchard had never seen such a horse. He must have stood a full sixteen hands. Every ounce of him was made for speed and strength in the best combination. There was the long forehead, which meant the rider's ease in controlling him; there was the long back of the racer, but not too long for weight-carrying purposes; the great breast spoke of the generous heart beneath; the head was poised with exquisite nicety. All this strength was superimposed upon legs slender and strong as hammered iron. There was not a mar in the black, except an irregular white splotch between the eyes, and a single white fetlock.

Such was Jerico. And at sight of him the crowd murmured in fear and admiration. He was like one of those rarely beautiful women who are always new.

At the murmur Jim Orchard looked back across the crowd. In his heart of hearts he despised them. They had come with divided will to see one of the two beaten—either the horse or the man—and he knew that they hardly cared which. To see the horse beaten into submission would be gratifying, but to see the rider thrown and broken would be infinitely more exciting. What right had they to come like spectators to a gladiatorial combat?

His heart went out with a sudden sympathy to the beautiful mustang. The saddle on his back and the heavily curbed bridle were a travesty. He should be shaking that glorious mane in the wind, at the head of a band of his mates. What right had they to imprison and torture him? With speed against speed, which was all that he was supposed to know, he had beaten them. Only by a trick they had taken him. The lesson of cunning and cruelty that they had taught him he now used against his captors. And Jim Orchard silently approved. Strangely he felt a kinship with this imprisoned beast. He was imprisoned, also—

153

blindfolded by a promise to a man—the love of a woman.

He climbed the high fence and dropped into the corral. "We'll have an even break," he said to the old Negro who stood near the head of the stallion. "Take the blindfold off Jerico. Take it off, I say," he repeated, as the other merely gaped at him.

The white-haired old fellow groaned. "Does this heah man knows what all he's talking about, Glory?" He bowed his head and addressed a fat-bodied, sleepy-eyed bull terrier beside him, and the dog twitched the stump of his tail.

"Don't act crazy, Orchard!" called someone from the mob. "You'll never get on that horse unless he's blindfolded!"

"Let him alone. Jim'll work it out his own way. He's going to teach us something new about horse-breaking." That was Garry Munn's voice.

Jim deliberately turned and smiled over the heads of the crowd into the face of Garry. This was another thing to be remembered.

He turned back and, at his repeated order, the Negro finally climbed up on the side of the fence and, leaning cautiously, jerked away the bandage from Jerico's eyes. The latter tossed his head to the light and at the same instant left the ground, bucked in mid-air, and came down with stiffly braced legs, before he seemed to realize that there was no rider in the saddle. Then he stood quivering with excitement and anger in the center of the corral, until he caught sight of Jim Orchard standing alone, unprotected by the fence that kept Jerico from that hated mass of faces.

He snorted once in amazement and suspicion—then lunged straight at the solitary stranger. From the crowd there went up a yell of horror—a familiar music to the ear of Jerico—he had heard it many a time when the would-be rider was flung like a stone from the saddle and crushed against the ground. So let it be with this man.

But Jim Orchard did not stir. All in a split part of a second he reviewed his life, knew he was a fool, and cursed his luck, because there was no escape from this tigerish devil of a horse. And then he stood his ground without lifting a hand and watched death come at him.

It came—and swerved aside. Jerico leaped away and stood beside the bars once more, snorting, stamping, flaunting his tail. Things that did not stir when he charged them were usually lifeless, like the post of a fence. And, if one rashly collided with such things, there was only a stunning repulse for a reward. Certainly, said the brute mind, that is a man, and yet he did not stir. A doubt came to Jerico. This was a man, and yet no man had ever approached him before on foot, unarmed with even the stinging whip.

Besides, the others, who had screamed a moment ago and stood so hushed, so terribly silent now, were protected by the fence. This creature must be different from the others.

He made a step toward Jim Orchard, paused, made another step, and then sprang away. The man had slowly raised his hand and now held it out in the immemorial sign of friendship and conciliation that even brute beasts learn sooner than any other human gesture. Jerico cocked his head and watched in amazement.

Then a voice began over the silence of the hundreds, a smooth, steady voice. It was an oddly fascinating voice, and it instantly convinced him that this was a new species—not a man at all. Other men yelled and made harsh sounds of fury, while they beat him with quirts and tore his tender sides with spurs. Yes, this creature was not a man at all. The sound of his voice took hold of the nerves of Jerico and soothed them and gave him queer reassurance.

But what was this? The creature was walking straight toward him.

Jerico flung himself away into the farthest corner like a flash and waited again, very curious. Behold, the man came toward him again, always speaking steadily, softly, his hand extended.

It was not altogether new. One other human being had seemed not dangerous to Jerico, and that was old Tom, the Negro. He had learned from Tom that it is not unpleasant to have a hand run down one's neck, or across the velvet of the nose. And the approach of this stranger bore with it infinite promises of pleasure, safety, protection from that horde of white, mute faces beyond the fence.

He began to tremble, more in curiosity than fear or, rather, with a mixture of both emotions. And now the man was close, closer. The hand moved out. Should he tear it with his strong teeth? No, there was no danger. There was no dreaded rope in those fingers. He waited, blinked, and then, as he had almost known, the fingertips trailed across his nose. A miracle!

A miracle, indeed, it seemed to the waiting throng when, after some breathless moments, they beheld the black stallion actually drop his nose on the shoulder of Jim Orchard and stare defiantly at the faces beyond the fence.

There was only one sound. It was the voice of old Tom, the Negro, saying in a sort of chant: "Glory be! Glory be!"

And still the crowd was incredulous. They would not believe their eyes as they saw Jim Orchard work his way to the side of the animal, test the stirrup, and put weight upon it with his hand. The stallion winced and turned his head with the ears flattened. His great teeth closed on the arm of Jim and crushed the flesh against the bone but, in spite of the torture, Orchard did

157

not vary the tone of his voice a jot. Presently the teeth relaxed their hold. There was a groan of relief from the crowd—a groan full of horror and tense excitement. In a way this was the most horrible horse-breaking that had ever been seen.

Finally the foot of Jim Orchard was in that stirrup, his weight grew heavier, and at length he raised himself slowly up, and up, swung his leg over, and settled into the stirrups. That familiar burden for one moment drove the stallion mad with fear and rage. He hurtled in the air and gave for ten seconds a hair-raising exhibition of bucking.

And then, with the shrieking of the delighted spectators in his ears, he stopped abruptly.

He was right. This was some other creature and not a man at all. In spite of his frantic efforts, no tearing steel points had been driven into his sides, no stinging whip had cut his flanks, no hoarse voice had bellowed curses at him.

Instead, the smooth, even voice had begun again—steadying, steadying, steadying. The sound of that voice fell like sleep upon the ragged nerves of Jerico. Someone near the fence yelled and waved a hat. Jerico tossed up his head and crouched for a leap.

"Gents!" rang the voice of Jim Orchard. "Another stunt like that and I out with my gun and start spraying lead. I mean it! You're going to give me and Jerico a fair chance to get acquainted. Show's over for the day!"

But before he dismounted, he glanced across to the door of the shack and saw the face of Sam Jordan convulsed with wonder and ugly malice.

VI

Until the very last act of that little drama Garry Munn had not stirred. For five minutes he had been praying silently. If Jerico had been susceptible to the influence of mental telepathy, he would certainly have smashed Jim Orchard to small bits. Instead, the miracle had happened, and Garry turned away and hurried back to the hotel. There he swung into his saddle, trotted to the outskirts of the town, and then rode at full speed out the road, deep in the dust which the unaccustomed traffic had churned up around the town.

Two miles of hard galloping, and he swung from the road down a cattle trail which brought him, almost at once, to a right-angled bend, and then to a full view of a little shack. There was a broad, perfectly level meadowland stretching away to the left, and across this smooth ground a midget of a man was galloping a long-legged bay. Garry Munn drew his own horse down to a walk and watched with a brightening eye. Yet the bay was not a horse to win the admiration of the ordinary cowpuncher. He was too long in the back, too thin of legs, too gaunt of neck, too meager of shoulders and hips to please men who look at a horse with an eye for his usefulness on long journeys and the heart-breaking labors of the roundup.

The bay was a horse that, it could be seen at a glance, needed the proverbial forty-acre lot to turn around in. Neither was his action imposing. He stood awkwardly. His trot was a spiritless shamble, his canter a loose-jointed, shuffling gait. But, when he began to run, there was a distinct difference. He thrust out his long neck, and the Roman-nosed head at the end of it. His little thin ear flagged back along his neck, the lengthy legs flung out in amazing strides, and the ground whirled under him with deceptive speed. He ran not with the jerky labor of a cow pony, but with jack-rabbit bounds, and he was far faster than he looked. Garry Munn eyed him with distinct favor. When the midget rider saw him, he brought the bay to a jolting trot that landed him in front of the shack.

"He's coming into shape," Garry said, joining the other.

The only reply was a brief grunt. The little man industriously set about removing the saddle and then began to rub the bay. He continued his ministrations with a sort of grim energy for a full twenty minutes, then, having tethered the horse in the lean-to beside the shack, he gave some attention to Garry.

"He ain't in shape. Not by a lot," he declared. "How do you expect me to get him in shape, running on plowed ground?"

"Plowed ground?" asked Garry Munn. "Why, Tim, I picked this place out because it's the smoothest ground around the town. You can't beat it anywhere."

"Smooth, eh?" demanded little Tim. "It's so rough that I ain't dared to let him out. I ain't been able to give Exeter his head, once."

"Wasn't he going full tilt a minute ago?" Garry asked admiringly.

"Him? Nothing like it! Now when Exeter . . ."

"Cut out that name. He's in this race as Long Tom. You'll spoil everything if you let that name drop."

"He's long enough, and the rules will find him a bit too long when he gets going. Only I wish I was down to weight."

"What's your weight now?"

"Clothes and all, maybe I tip the old beam around a hundred and fifteen."

He was well under five feet tall, with a withered skull face, a pinched neck, and diminutive legs. All his strength lay in the abnormally long arms and the sturdy shoulders.

"Why, Hogan," Garry Munn said, "that's a

161

good thirty pounds lighter than any other rider."

"Maybe it is, maybe it isn't. But Exeter . . . Long Tom, I mean . . . is cut out for fly-weight racing. Put him in with ninety pounds, and he's a whirlwind. Stick more'n a hundred on him, and he don't like it. He ain't got the underpinning for weight."

"It's only a mile," said Garry eagerly. "He'll surely last that?"

"Easy, if I don't have to stretch him out. How's the black? What come of that Castor fellow?"

"He's smashed. One arm and both legs busted up."

The little man sighed. "You owe me a lot for that little piece of work," he said gloomily.

"You'll find I'll pay," said Garry. "How'd you fix it?"

"I just sneaked around until I found out what saddle they were going to use on the black. Then I fixed the saddle." He grinned briefly with malicious pleasure, and then his expression sobered. "What happened?"

"Jerico went mad. That's all. He smashed Bud to pieces. I never saw such a devil when it comes to bucking."

"Well, now that we got the black out of the race, I ain't worrying. I've timed the others, and they're a cinch."

Garry delivered his bad news. "Tim, Jerico is in the race again."

Tim Hogan blinked. "A daredevil named Orchard rode Jerico just a while ago and got on with him, as if Jerico were an old pack horse. We're in for it. How fast can the black go?"

"How fast? Too fast!"

"How far did you see him run?"

"It ain't what the clock told me. It's what my eyes told me. That Jerico has a racing heart. You'll find him doing about twice better in a race than he does in practice. Well, put Exeter on a good fast track with ninety pounds up, a little racing luck, and he'd trim all the Jericos that ever stepped on plates. But Exeter has to pack twenty-five pounds more'n he likes, and I don't know what he'll do. He may quit on me. Chief, you got to get Jerico out of the way, if you want to win that race!"

Garry Munn cursed softly and fluently.

"It can't be done, now. You don't know this fellow Orchard. He has an eye like a hawk's and, if he finds anyone around tampering with a bridle, or saddle, he'll fill the man full of lead. That's Orchard's way. He shoots first and asks his questions of the coroner. But there's one thing to help us, Tim. That's the weight. Orchard is a big fellow. He must weigh a hundred and eighty . . . thirty pounds more than Castor."

"A hundred and eighty?" asked Tim Hogan cheerfully. "Why that'd anchor another Salvator."

"It'll beat Jerico, then?"

But Tim had grown thoughtful. "You can't always tell about a horse," he declared. "No way of figuring whether a horse will be a hog for carrying the weight or not. And Jerico looks like an iron horse. Never saw such legs. He could carry a ton, from his looks. A hundred and eighty would break Exeter's back, but Jerico might dance with it. It ain't likely . . . but then you never can tell. You got to fix that horse so's he can't run if you want to be sure of the race."

"I've got to win," declared Munn. "They'll give me odds of three to one against Long Tom, and I've raked together thousands for the plunge. They don't like the looks of Tom. They think he'll break to pieces when he starts running. I can get any odds I want against him."

"What'd happen if they knew Exeter was off a race track, with a record of wins as long as my arm? What'd happen if they knew I was a jockey, that I don't own the horse, and that you brought me on for this clean-up? I've been sizing up the boys around here, guns and all, and I just been wondering what would happen to us both, Mister Munn, if they had a hunch about what's happening."

"They'd string us up to the nearest tree and fill us full of lead," said Garry quickly. "That's their way."

Tim Hogan shook himself. "It don't bother me none," he declared. "I was in the ring before I started riding a string. I won't get cold feet. But say, Mister Munn, why don't you fix this rider . . . this Orchard . . . as long as you can't fix the horse."

"Fix him? How?"

"Get him to pull Jerico in the race."

Garry started, but then shook his head. "You don't know Jim Orchard. Besides, I couldn't approach him."

"You don't have to. I'll do it. I've done it before. They all got a price, if you can go high enough."

"I wonder," Garry said, sweating with anxiety. "Nine chances out of ten he'd throw you out the window."

"I don't pack much weight . . . I'd light easy."

"It can't be done."

"It can be done. They all got a price. How high could I go with him?"

His confidence was contagious.

"You could go to the sky," said Garry Munn. "Why, if Jerico's in the race, the men around here will bet everything down to their socks. I know half a dozen ranchers who'd go ten thousand apiece on Jerico if they could find anyone to cover their money. There's an idea around these parts that Jerico can't be beaten by anything in the shape of horseflesh." He became excited. "If Jerico runs, there'll be a hundred thousand . . . maybe more . . . in sight to bet on him."

"Then cop it. Cop it, Mister Munn. But where do I come in?"

"If you work the deal, Tim, it means a thousand flat to you, and ten percent of everything I make."

"And how'd I be sure you'd come through?"

"I've never gone back on a promise in my life."

The little man watched him with a peculiar glance of scorn. "I guess you ain't," he admitted at last. "Besides, you don't dare go back on me. How high with this Jim Orchard?"

"A thousand, five thousand, ten thousand . . . anything you want. There's a better way. Get him to bet his money on Exeter."

"Chief," declared the jockey with a grin, "you learn fast."

VII

As for Jim Orchard, when he swung down gently from the saddle on Jerico, there was a relieved groan of appreciation and wonder, but he paid no further attention to the crowd.

"He's just putting off your little party!" one of the men called warningly to Orchard.

And perhaps he was, but something told Orchard that for the first time a man had stepped into the confidence of the black stallion. After all, had not many a stranger thing than this episode been told of horses? And was it not possible that

Jerico, having battled and hated his would-be masters for so long, had finally decided that one, at least, might be accepted on trust? Jim Orchard decided to take the chance.

All his life he had done nothing but play some such chance—whether he were gambling on the turn of a card, or the dependable qualities in a man. Deliberately he raised the stirrup and stirrup flap and put them across the saddle. Then he commenced to work at the knots of the cinches. The moment he had brought them loose and drew on the cinch straps to free them, the head of Jerico swung on him again. But this time the stallion merely bared his teeth without touching Orchard. The ears that were flattened against the horse's neck pricked a little as he watched Orchard loose the cinches and remove the saddle.

It was the first time that Jerico had seen this done. Hitherto he had been roped and blinded for saddling or unsaddling, to keep his murderous, striking hoofs still. Now he discovered that no matter what hateful agency put the saddle upon him, this man, this stranger of the gentle voice, could remove it. Jerico was not quite sure of any of this, but his misty animal brain was moving faintly toward the conviction that the man was at least not harmful. At the first suspicious move he was ready to scatter the brains of Jim Orchard in the dust of the corral. In the meantime, his would be a policy of watchful waiting.

Orchard was keen enough to sense what went on behind the suspicious eyes of the horse. No matter how well he had succeeded so far, he took care to make every motion slow, gentle, and kept up a steady stream of talk. Then with the saddle over the crook of his arm, he walked calmly out of the corral, his back actually turned upon the man-killer! His hand was wrung on every side the moment the gate closed behind him.

It was: "Good old Jim, I sure was saying good bye to you for a minute or two."

"That's the nerve, Jim."

"You win, old boy."

"Tame the lions, Orchard."

But Jim Orchard wondered if every one of them was not just a trifle disappointed. It would have been sufficiently thrilling to see either man or horse beaten, but this compromise, which left dignity and physical soundness to both man and beast, was a wretched compromise. Jim hung the saddle on its peg in the barn. The crowd had already scattered, now that the crisis had passed. There was only the grinning old Negro, Tom, and the fat bull terrier that trailed at his heels, almost bumping his nose against them. No matter where Tom turned, the dog made it an earnest practice to keep directly behind him.

"I knowed it all the time, Mistah Orchard," averred Tom. "Trouble with all them others was they was sure dead set on breaking Jerico's heart. For why? Had poor ol' Jerico done 'em any harm? No, suh, that he hadn't. But I take off my hat to you, suh. It took a brave man to find out that Jerico weren't no murderer, but jus' an honest horse that had been taught all wrong."

"I hear you've got on pretty well with Jerico yourself," said Jim Orchard.

"Couldn't be better, suh. When I first come, Jerico he takes a couple of swipes at ol' Tom's head. But he missed, praise the Lawd, and pretty soon he find out that Tom ain't doin' him no harm, jus' foolin' aroun' and feedin' him and bringin' him out to water. He's been mighty afraid, that's all that's been wrong with ol' Jerico, Mistah Orchard."

"You broke the ice for me," said Jim. "If it hadn't been for what you'd taught him, he'd've busted me into little bits. I'm going to saddle him up myself later on, when there isn't a crowd to watch, and we'll try a canter down the road together."

"He's a wise horse, Mistah Orchard. He'll know you same's if you raised him from a colt, by morning. All Jerico needs is just to make up his mind about sumthin'. Look at ol' Glory, now. Jerico wouldn't have my dog aroun' for a long time. And now they're jus' plumb friendly. Go talk to Jerico, Glory!"

Old Glory, hearing this order, cast a skulking

glance at Jim Orchard and then slunk toward the corral. Once outside the barn he seemed to gather courage. He trotted straight for the stallion and, rising on his hind legs under the nose of the horse, barked at him softly. Jerico in answer deliberately and gently tipped old Glory over with a push of his nose. But Glory came up again and danced, with all the agility his fat allowed, around the great horse. Jerico followed, pretending anger, striking gently with his forefeet, wide of the mark.

"Look there, now!" exclaimed Tom delighted. "I ask you, Mistah Orchard, is that the way a man-killin' horse ought to act? Why, Jerico's plumb gentle, once he gets to know you. It's the cussin' and the whips that he's been fightin', not the men."

"You're right," agreed Jim Orchard, amazed at that dumb show in the corral. "You're right from the first. But what's the matter with that dog, Tom? Has somebody been beating him?"

"They's a long story about ol' Glory, Mistah Orchard. You see him sneakin' aroun' like he didn't have no soul of his own? Well, suh, I seen him the best fightin' dog that ever was. Plumb wild, ol' Glory was. His master used to keep him half starved to have him wild, and then he'd bet on Glory to his last nickel . . . and always Glory won, chewin' up the other dog sump'n terrible to talk of. But one time Mistah Simpson . . . that was him that owned Glory . . . done le' him go without no food for a long time. Po' white trash, that man was, suh! An' he put ol' Glory all weak and tremblin' into the ring. Shucks, Glory would've made jus' two mouthfuls of the other dog, if he'd been strong. But he was like a little puppy afraid of the cold that day . . . he was so weak.

"He got chewed up scandalous, suh, Glory did that day. They got the other dog off him just in time, and after that Glory ain't been no good. They fatted him up and got him strong and put him back ag'in' another dog, suh, but Glory jus' got down in the corner an' wouldn't come out. His heart had been broke, suh, you see? An' ever since he's been like this. Jus' draggin' aroun' dodgin' eyes when folks look at him. Even ol' Tom can't get Glory to look him in the eye, but he keeps skulkin' and draggin' and bumpin' his nose ag'in' my heels, suh."

"But why do you keep him, Tom?"

"You git sorter fond of a dog, suh. But always I keep dreamin' and thinkin' of the dog that ol' Glory used to be and the dog he might've been . . . if the heart hadn't been plumb busted in him, suh."

"Tom," said Jim Orchard, much moved, "you're a good sort. And you're right, I figure. I've known horses the same way. Particular the wild ones. Beat 'em once and they're no good ever after. I'll wager that Jerico might be that sort of a horse. What do you think?"

"They ain't no doubt. Beat him once and he'll go aroun' hangin' his head . . . an' any boy could git on him and thump him with his bare heels."

Orchard sighed. "Kind of a responsibility, a horse like that. How much do you think Sam Jordan would be wanting for Jerico?"

The Negro shrugged his shoulders and peered up into the face of Orchard with a timid smile. "I don't think no man has got money to buy him from Mistah Jordan, suh."

"Why not? Sam isn't rich."

"Well, suh . . ." Tom paused.

"I won't repeat what you say. Go ahead, Tom."

"Ever get stung by wasps, Mistah Orchard, and go back to the rest of the boys and say nothin' about it and get 'em to come and walk over the same hole in the ground to see what'd happen to 'em?"

There was a pause during which the whole meaning of this sunk into the brain of Jim Orchard. He had had the ugly suspicion concerning Sam Jordan before, and he could not forget the singular expression on the face of the cripple at the moment when Jerico stopped bucking. It was a bad affair from the beginning to end.

He glanced out the barn door and saw old Glory trotting back to his master. At that moment a cowpuncher sauntered past. The terrier crouched till his belly touched the ground, skidded deftly around the stranger, and then raced for dear life until he was safe behind the shoes of Tom.

Jim Orchard had seen enough. He was filled with an insane desire to find that former master of the fighting bull terrier and beat the brutal fellow to a pulp, until he became as cringing a coward as he had made his dog.

So he walked to the front of the shack and stopped beside Sam Jordan. There was no hint of friendliness in the glance that the cripple cast at him. There was a smile, to be sure, but it was so forced and bespoke so much hidden malice, that it chilled the tall puncher's blood.

"That was a pretty clever trick," said Sam Jordan, still smiling. "What'd you do? Dope Jerico first? Get old Tom to mix something in his feed before you tried him out?"

"Did I have a chance to get at Tom before I tried to ride Jerico?"

Sam Jordan thought a moment. "I dunno," he admitted grudgingly. "It don't seem no ways possible."

"How about selling Jerico, Sam?"

"Selling him? Not in a thousand years!"

"But what's he worth to you, man?"

The grin of Sam Jordan became a horrible caricature of mirth. "He's worth . . . this." With a slow, inclusive gesture, he indicated the crippled

173

legs. "I've paid for him with my legs. Do you think you could raise that price, maybe, Jim?"

"But what use is he to you, man?"

"I dunno. I'm just sort of used to having him around. You planning on turning him into a family pet, Jim? Just keep watching your step, partner. Jerico ain't through by no means."

"But I've thought of this, Sam. By the time I have him tame enough to ride in the race tomorrow he'll be pretty well broken. Besides, I don't think the thousand is worth the chance I'm taking."

"You ain't calling the bargain off, Jim?" asked the cripple, growing suddenly conciliatory. His expression made Orchard think of the spider that sees the fly creeping off beyond his reach. He decided to see what bluffing would do.

"I'll stick to the bargain, if you'll let me make another deal with you. Suppose I take all the chances, and I'm able to ride Jerico in the race? Well, then, name a reasonable price and let me buy him when the race is over."

"No chance, Jim."

"Then I'm through. Try out somebody else for your jockey."

"Wait!"

"You've heard me, Sam. I mean it."

"Take a price after the race is finished?" Sam Jordan argued, evidently turning the proposition in his mind and deciding that there was very little chance of Jim Orchard or any other man staying on the back of the stallion through the excitement that was bound to seize the mustang during a contest with other horses.

"Name a good round figure, Sam."

"One thousand for Jerico, then, if you stick on him through the whole race."

"A thousand it is."

They shook hands, and the fingers of Sam Jordan were bloodless and cold to the touch.

VIII

Turning his back on Jordan, Jim Orchard strode off down the street. He had taken on a new obligation. To the original five thousand which had been his goal, and which he now had an excellent chance of winning, provided Jerico was first in the race, there was added the purchase price of the stallion. The total he needed was six thousand dollars.

Again he was glad that Sue could not know. He had already placed his chance of happiness under the danger of a mortgage. What would she think if she knew that he had admitted a brute beast—a horse—on the same plane with her?

He turned on his heel. Jerico was still visible. He had pressed forward against the fence of the corral, and he was watching his late rider disappear. He even tossed up his head and whinnied when he saw Jim turn. The latter remained for a moment staring, a lump growing in his throat. Then he resumed his walk.

I've got to have that horse, Orchard thought conclusively. Then his mind turned happily to Sue Hampton. Of course, she would not have had the courage to come to see the riding and, though she must have learned of the outcome of his daring by this time, no doubt she would be glad to see him and be reassured that all was well. He went to her house.

She was on the little verandah with a heap of silky stuff in her lap and a basket beside her. She raised her head and watched him coming up the path. When she saw him, she laid aside the sewing and folded her hands, and Jim Orchard knew that he was distinctly out of favor. Another girl in such a mood would have pretended not to see him. But it was one of Sue's peculiarities that she made no pretenses. She was as inexorable with herself as she was with others. He had known her to go out of her way to make quaint confessions of wrong thoughts that had been in her mind, after she had been proved wrong. But the terrible part of this was that she more or less expected others to treat her as she treated them. Unfortunately she expected the qualities of a saint in an ordinary cowpuncher.

It was one of the things that made Orchard love

her; it was also one of the things that kept him at arm's length and gave him, occasionally, a little touch of dread. Today it made him a little more swaggering. He tried to bluff his way through.

"Well," he greeted her, "you see everything's all right?"

It was always wonderful to see her brighten. "Then you're not going to ride Jerico?"

"But, Sue, I've already ridden him."

"I mean in the race tomorrow?"

"But he's safe enough. Haven't I just finished trying him out?"

"I heard about it," said the girl. "They told me how you . . . almost tempted him to kill you."

"It was the only thing to do," said Jim, growing sullen as he saw what position she was going to take. "Other fellows have fought Jerico . . . plenty of them . . . and I thought I'd try persuasion."

"I think I know," she answered with that deadly softness. "There was such a crowd . . . you had to do something to thrill them. So you forgot about your own safety . . . you forgot about me . . . you gave the crowd a show."

The injustice of it rankled in him. "Do you think that I'm low enough for that?"

It was her turn to flush with anger. "You shouldn't have said that, Jim. But if we start out with misunderstanding . . ."

"You're going to threaten to give that ring back to me again?" he asked coldly.

"I think it would be better."

Jim Orchard for the moment almost forgot that he was talking to a woman—the woman he loved. He put his boot on the edge of the verandah, dropped his elbow on his knee, and lectured her with a raised forefinger.

"You'll keep that ring till the end of tomorrow," he said fiercely. "It makes me tired, Sue, the way you women act. A gent might think that honor didn't have nothing to do with women. It's just for men only. I give you a promise and I got to stick to it to the bitter end. You gave me a promise that you're going to stick by me until tomorrow night. Now you welch and try to get out of your promise, but it doesn't work with me. You're going to keep that ring, Sue. And if I've got the money by tomorrow night, you're going to marry me. Don't you forget it in the meanwhile."

Then he turned his back on her and strode away without further ado, rage straightening his shoulders. Sue Hampton gazed after him as though a new star had swum into her heaven—a blazing comet dazzling her. She sat for a long time with her sewing unheeded, while the day faded and the darkness came. Before the end she was smiling tenderly to herself.

There's something about Jim, she mused, *something different.*

The "something different" made Jim stamp his

way up the stairs of the hotel to his room and fling himself on his cot. In the nick of time he recalled a comforting remark that a friend of his had once made.

No man that's worth his salt ever understands his womenfolk, really. The point is women are like mules . . . they go by opposites.

This reflection cheered Jim Orchard vastly, and he was about to go downstairs for his dinner when a knock came at the door, and a little man with a fleshless face of excessive ugliness stood before him.

"You're Jim Orchard?"

"Yes."

"You're interested in the race?"

"I'm riding Jerico."

"Can you give me half an hour, Mister Orchard?"

"Why, sure."

He was putting his hat on as he spoke. Of course it might be some sort of a trap, but the little man was reckless, indeed, if he were trying to bait a trap for Jim Orchard. He followed down the stairs and stepped into a buckboard beside the other.

"I'm Tim Hogan," said the small man, and not once did he open his lips after that, but sent his span of horses at full speed across the town and over the dusty road. They turned to the left after a time and bumped over a cattle trail, the driver skillfully picking his way in spite of the dimness of the moonlight. When they reached a little shack, before which a tall bay horse stood saddled, they stopped and climbed down.

"Now," said Tim Hogan, "have you got a stopwatch?"

"Nope."

"I have. Here it is. You take it. It works like this," he explained deftly. He went on: "It's four hundred yards from the stump yonder to that white rock. Want to pace it?"

"I'll take your word," Jim Orchard said, wondering if he had fallen into the hands of a maniac.

"Here goes."

Tim Hogan climbed up the lofty side of the bay and dropped into the saddle. He rode to the stump.

"Now raise your left arm."

Jim obeyed.

"When you drop that arm, I'm going to start the bay for the rock . . . when I start the bay, you start the watch."

At last Orchard understood. "Good."

He raised his arm, and as he did so the rider raised himself a little in his short stirrups and threw his weight well over the withers of the horse. He was bowed so that his body was straightened out at right angles to the perpendicular.

"Go!" exclaimed Jim, dropping his arm, and with the word the long bay gathered himself and flung out.

He was going at full speed in half a dozen jumps—and such jumps! The flying legs well-nigh disappeared in that dim light. It seemed that the rakish body and the long, snaky neck were shooting through space with no visible means of support. The dark outline whipped past the white rock, and Jim stopped the watch.

He raised it high to read the hand in the dim light, and in this position he remained as one turned to stone. So Tim Hogan found him when he jogged back on Exeter, alias Long Tom. He dismounted, grinning broadly, but the dimness concealed his exultation.

"What do you think?" he asked.

Without a word Jim Orchard returned the stopwatch to the jockey. "A quarter of a mile is not a mile," he said.

"Never anything truer that I've heard say," returned Tim. "And the longer the distance the better for the horse with the lightest weight up. I guess that's straight, Mister Orchard."

"Hmm," said Jim.

"Jerico never saw the day he could step a quarter as fast as that one . . . and he never will," said Tim.

"What's the main idea behind all this?" Jim asked suspiciously.

"The main idea is that Long Tom is going to win tomorrow."

"Why bring me out in the night to show that to me? Why not win my money and tell me after the race is run?"

"Look here," said Tim, "I'm laying my cards on the table."

"That's the way to talk to me. Now come out with it."

"Well, sir, I've put up a lot of hard cash on this race, and tomorrow I'm going to get down a lot more."

"Well?"

"What do you think of the chances of the rest of the ponies against Long Tom . . . eh?"

"Jerico . . ."

"Leave out Jerico."

"Leave out Jerico and there's no race. They'll be too far back of Long Tom . . . the rest of 'em . . . to eat his dust."

"You've said a mouthful, general. With Jerico out it'd be just an exercise gallop for Long Tom. But the rest of the boys around here don't know it. They ain't seen what Ex- . . . Long Tom can do. They haven't any idea. They figure his long legs will get all tied up in knots, and he'll break down inside a hundred yards. But he ain't going to get tied up. He's going to win."

"You've said that plenty of times, partner. What's the point?"

"The point is the rest of the gents around here are going to plunge on Jerico. They got an idea that nothing can beat that horse. They're going to give me big odds on Long Tom, and I'm going to cover every cent they'll put up. Besides, I've got backing. I've got a backer who's investing every cent he can rake together . . . going into this up to his eyes. Now you can figure for yourself that he wants to make this a safe race, eh?"

"That's easy to follow."

"And there's only one danger . . . that's Jerico. You see, I'm putting the cards on the table."

"I see."

"What we want to be sure of is that no matter what happens to the rest of the horses, and no matter how fast Long Tom has to run to beat 'em, he won't have to worry about Jerico."

"But you've already tried to show me, partner, that you ain't a bit afraid of Jerico."

"Have I? Well, we are afraid, a little. At least he's what keeps our game from being a sure thing. Nobody knows just how fast Jerico can run if he's put to it, or how far he can carry the weight. Now, our proposition is to make sure that Jerico finishes behind Long Tom. That is, if Tom's leading. Mind you, if one of the other ponies gets out in front, then you're free to let go with Jerico and win if you can. But as long as Tom's in front you're to keep back with the black. Is that clear?"

"I hear you talk," said Jim Orchard, "but I don't get you. It ain't no ways possible that you figure I'd pull Jerico? That I'd keep him from doing his best?"

"Look here," replied Tim Hogan, "I ask you man to man . . . do you think Jerico can beat Long Tom?"

"Man to man, I don't think he can. But I don't know."

"You don't think so, and neither do I. But I simply want to make it a sure thing. I'm putting up too much coin to take a chance, no matter how small the chance is. Orchard, I am asking you to pull Jerico."

Something came into the face of Orchard that made the other spring away.

"Easy!" he cried. "Easy, Orchard! Jerico hasn't a chance in a hundred. I'm just asking you to wipe out even that hundredth chance. And I'm talking business. I'm talking money."

"Get into that buckboard," Jim Orchard said hoarsely, "and drive me back to town."

"Do you mean that? But I say, I'm talking money. I'm talking a thousand dollars, man, if you'll pull Jerico on the hundredth chance."

"Climb into that buckboard and drive me back. If you had a gun, Hogan, I'd do more than talk to you."

"I'm talking two thousand . . . three thousand dollars, Orchard. Are you deaf?"

184

"Deaf as a stone."

"Four thousand. I'll do better. Give me what money you have, and I'll get it down for you on Long Tom at three to one. How does that sound to you?"

"Hogan, for the last time, will you drive me back, or do I drive back alone?"

Tim Hogan climbed obediently into the buckboard. Not once on the return trip did he speak, feeling the silent loathing and scorn of the big man. But when Jim Orchard climbed down near the hotel, the jockey leaned far out across the wheel and whispered: "Think it over, Orchard. I'll expect an answer. Think it over. Easy money, man. Easy money. Three dollars for one!" He put the whip to the mustangs, and the buckboard jumped away from the curse of Jim Orchard.

IX

The cowpuncher felt that the matter was closed the moment the wagon whirled out of sight around the corner but, oddly enough, the silence that followed was more tempting than the voice of the jockey. It was the first time in his life that anyone had ever attempted to bribe him. Ordinarily he would have made his revolver reply to such an offer, but one could not draw a weapon on an unarmed man, and it was impossible to

185

use fists on a fellow of the size of Tim Hogan.

The heart of Jim Orchard was heavy. He pushed through a crowd on the verandah—a crowd that wanted to tell him, one by one, how much they thought of the nerve he had shown in the riding of Jerico that day. He broke through them and entered the hotel.

To those men on the verandah the race was already run and won. They would bet their last dollars on Jerico, for had they not heard how he had been run? Were there not men at the rodeo who had actually taken part in the chase of the wild mustang, and who had seen him wear out horse after horse in the relay that followed Jerico?

But Jerico was beaten. He was as sure of it as if he had actually seen the gallant black pounding down the homestretch, behind the flaunting tail of the long-legged bay. Nothing equine that he had ever seen had moved with the speed of Long Tom. Of course there were unknown possibilities in Jerico. And in a longer race—five or six miles, say—in spite of the greater weight he had to carry, he would undoubtedly break the heart of Long Tom and win as he pleased. But for a single flash of speed—a single mile of sprinting—what chance had Jerico against the long legs and the flyweight rider of the bay?

Jim Orchard dragged a chair up to the window of his room and looked gloomily into the night.

He looked forward to the beating of Jerico as to a personal shame and mortification. There was something wrong about it. It should not be allowed. Take Long Tom in the open desert with a day's ride ahead, and what use would he be? And, therefore, was it not bitterer than words could tell that he should be allowed to win fame and name by outstepping the staunch Jerico over a single mile?

There was a sudden outburst of noise, a chorus of voices, shouts, laughter, mocking yells, spilling across the verandah. What was it?

"On what? On Long Tom?"

"What horse is that?"

"Never seen him."

"I have, it's a bay with legs almost as long as I'm tall."

Then, as the hubbub died away, he made out a clear, strong voice: "All right, boys, have your laugh. But I think those long legs can carry the horse over the ground. What's more, I'll back up what I say with money."

It was the voice of Garry Munn.

"But you're nutty, Munn. Jerico's in the race! And he's like a lamb with Jim Orchard in the saddle. Didn't you see Jim ride the black today?"

"I saw it. Still I have some faith in Long Tom. What odds will you give me, chief?"

"Anything you want."

"Five to one."

"Five to one what?"

"Five thousand to one thousand!"

"Take you, Garry!"

The hubbub roared again. It became a blur, blotting the mind of Jim Orchard.

Garry Munn was the backer of Tim Hogan and the bay horse? Garry Munn was the man who was prepared to plunge up to the eyes? Jim bowed his head, for this was more than he could bear. The very day which was to see him fail to make good in making six thousand, which he had set his heart on possessing, this was to be the day of all days for Garry Munn. The very day which saw him fail to win either Sue Hampton or the black stallion, this was the day which was to give Garry Munn a real fortune—and Sue Hampton as well. About the girl, Jim was perfectly certain. She had waited too long. When she finally left him, she would go to the man who could offer her all that Jim lacked.

Then, into the confusion of his mind, came the voice of the little man with the withered face as he leaned out across the wheel of the buckboard. What was it he had said with so much confidence?

You'll think it over. Easy money, man. Easy money. Three dollars for one.

Of course it was easy money. It was more than easy. It was picking the gold out of the street. What difference did it make? Garry Munn would

188

never bet on a rash chance, and yet he was apparently backing Long Tom with thousands. And whether Jerico were pulled or not in the race, he had not a chance in ten of winning. Why not get in on the clean-up? Why not wager his two thousand at odds of three or four to one? Then, even if Jerico were beaten, he would win both the girl and the horse. Was it double-crossing those men who were wagering their very boots on Jerico?

Forget them, Jim Orchard thought savagely to himself, as this thought came home to him. *The world owes me something!*

On that thought he stuck. The world did, indeed, owe him something. Tomorrow should be his collection day. There might be some pangs of conscience afterward, but in the end Sue Hampton and Jerico would certainly salve those wounds. The babble had increased on the verandah.

"Wait a minute! One at a time!"

Garry Munn was fighting them off. They were wild with joy at the thought of putting a bet on Jerico. They were offering any odds he would take. Five, seven, ten to one.

It was too much for Jim Orchard.

He counted out the two thousand that made up his worldly fortune, scribbled a brief note which he stuffed into the mouth of the bag and, going down to the back of the hotel, found and saddled his horse and galloped to the shack of Tim Hogan. He kicked open the door without dismounting.

"Hogan!"

The little man with the withered face sauntered out to meet him. "I knew . . . ," he began.

"Take this and be hanged," said Orchard. Flinging down the bag, he wheeled his horse and spurred away.

As for Tim Hogan, he picked up the bag and opened it gingerly. His face lighted at the sight of the contents, and then he drew out the paper. He stood for a long time looking down at it. Finally he crumpled it again and dropped it into its former place.

"I didn't think he'd come around," Tim declared. "Didn't really think it."

He added joyously after a time: "But I guess they all got their price. Every one of 'em's got the tag on if you can only hit the right figure."

He was not half an hour alone before a second horseman galloped to his door.

"He's changed his mind," said Tim Hogan, almost happily.

But it was Garry Munn. He came in pale with excitement. "What's happened?" he asked. "Anything happen?"

"That," Tim said dryly, and pointed to the little sack of money.

"From Orchard? He's come through?"

"He has."

"We're to bet this on Long Tom?"

"We are."

Garry Munn shouted with relief and joy: "I knew it'd work!"

"What you done?"

"When you told me that Orchard had turned you down, I made up my mind to try a little bluff. I went to the verandah of the hotel and started betting on Long Tom to win."

"Before you knew Orchard would pull Jerico?"

"Sure. I was playing for Jim. I knew he'd hear me and get to thinking that Tom was sure to win no matter what he does."

"And Tom will win."

"Aye, but we can't take chances. They went mad when they heard that there was actually money out against Jerico. They gave me any odds I could ask. I didn't get much down. I let them waste time talking and making a noise to reach the ears of Orchard. All I bet was a few hundred . . . at anything from five to one to ten to one. Think of that! And it hooked him?"

"He came riding up a half hour ago and threw down that." Tim pointed at Orchard's money bag.

"Why, you fool, aren't you pleased?"

"I s'pose so. But it means one more good man gone to the bad. You won't hear me cheer. I've seen too much of it."

"But suppose something happens to Long Tom? Suppose he don't win? I'm ruined, Tim, because

I'm going to plunge in this up to the eyes. I'm going to soak every cent I can get my hands on into this race." He broke off as he drew out the paper that was in the mouth of the money bag.

"What's here?" Then he read aloud:

> Here you are, Hogan. Bet this on Long Tom for me.

He repeated that message, a smile slowly growing on his face.

"Well?" asked Tim Hogan. "Anything mysterious about that?"

But Garry Munn slowly spread and closed into a fist the fingers of one hand, as though he were strangling a creature of thin air.

"I've got him," he said.

"Got what?"

"He'll get paid the money he wins . . . and long odds at that, as pat as I can get for him. But he loses everything else."

"What?"

"His honor, Tim, and his girl!"

X

Fortunately for his own self-esteem, Garry Munn did not see the cynical smile with which Tim Hogan greeted his last speech. Tim had long since buried the last of his own scruples and could not even remember the long-distant day when he had decided to get along in the world minus the burden of a sense of honor. In his palmy times on the track he had done everything from artistically "roughing" the most dangerous of his competitors to cleverly "pocketing" or "pulling" his own mount.

He had made a great deal of money in this manner and had always been clever enough to keep away from suspicion. But for the very reason that he had decided to do without moral scruples in his own life, Tim was the keener critic of the morals of others. There was something highly repulsive to him in the apparent good nature of Garry Munn and the real, cold unscrupulousness which underlay the surface appearances.

Unaware of the scorn which was sneering behind his back, Garry went out from the shack singing gaily, and he took his way straight back to the town and then to the house of Sue Hampton. In the old days he had never paid much attention to Sue. Indeed, it was not until Jim Orchard took her up that Garry wakened to her possibilities. But he had long since formed such a habit of trying to get the same things that Jim Orchard wanted that when Jim seriously courted a woman, it seemed perfectly natural for Garry to desire the same girl.

He never pretended to understand Sue. But, next to his own fortunes, he loved her as much as he was able to love anything. And the pleasure of beating out Jim Orchard in this most important of competitions would suffice to sweeten an entire married life, he felt.

Before he knocked at her door he composed himself. In his hand he carried that sack of Orchard's money with which he was to destroy forever Jim's chances with the girl. In his mind he carried a convincing story. When he had arranged the details, he tapped. The lamp was picked up in the sitting room. He saw the light slant across the window and fade. Then the crack around the front door became an edging of light. The door was opened by Sue herself, who stood back, shading the lamp to keep the glare out of her eyes. It seemed to Garry Munn that the fingers of that hand were transparent.

"Is there anyone with you?" he asked.

"No one."

"Then come out on the verandah, Sue. I've got something to tell you. You don't mind me calling as late as this?"

"Of course not."

She disappeared and joined him at once in the semi-darkness. He was glad to have that sheltering dark, for from the first he had never been entirely at ease, so long as the grave, quiet eyes of the girl could probe his face. The lamplight, he felt, would have been an ally for Jim Orchard. The darkness, on the other hand, would be an ally for Garry Munn. He struck at once into the heart of his subject, because he knew that she was too clever to be fooled by his diplomacy.

"Sue," he said, "I've got a mighty ugly job, tonight. Before I get through talking you'll know I'm the best friend you've got in the world, or else you'll think I'm a hound. Shall I go ahead?"

"I don't know," answered the smooth voice of Sue Hampton. "Of course I won't know till I hear."

That was a characteristic speech, he felt. It would also be characteristic for Sue to suspend judgment to the very end of his story. He felt that he must prepare her.

"Well, we'll start supposing. Suppose you had a friend you thought a lot of . . . and that friend had another friend he thought a lot of . . ."

"I'm getting the friends all mixed up, Garry."

He blurted out impatiently: "It's about Jim Orchard!"

There was a long pause. He was not so sure that he was glad to have darkness. He would have given a good deal to be able to make out more than the blur of her features.

"Well?" she said at length.

"I've never bluffed with you, Sue," he went on. "I guess you know where I stand."

"Just what do you mean?"

This coolness was always a dash of water in his face.

"I mean you know my attitude toward you."

She hesitated just a trifle. "I think you've acted as if . . . as if you're a firm friend of mine, Garry. Is that what you mean?"

"Nothing more than a friend?"

"Yes," she admitted willingly enough, "more than a friend."

"And it hasn't bothered you to have me around so much?"

"I don't know just what all this leads to, Garry."

"Nothing that'll embarrass you, Sue. I'll give you my word."

"Then . . . of course, it hasn't bothered me. I like you a lot, Garry. Partly for reasons that aren't reasons. Partly because you're so clean."

He winced. "That's fine to hear. It gives me courage to go ahead and take chances with what's to come. But in the first place you admit that I've never tried to force myself on you, Sue. I've just gone on being fond of you for quite a time now, and never asking any return, never expecting anything? Is that true?"

"I think it is, Garry."

"Because I've taken it for granted that you belong to Jim Orchard."

She paused again. And he was glad of it. "No woman belongs to a man, until they're married."

"Not even then, really, Sue."

"Oh, yes. After a marriage . . . that means a giving without any reservation . . . a giving of the whole heart, Garry. But I don't think a man can understand."

"The point is this. You know that I've never made any pretenses about you. I've never asked any return. I've never had any hopes. Do you know why? Because I've always thought Jim was worthy of you."

"Go on," said a faint voice.

"Tonight it's different."

He had ventured everything on the blunt statement; he half expected that she would order him to leave. But she made no murmur of a reply.

"I'm going to tell you why. It may seem like coming behind Jim's back. I'm sorry, but I don't see any other way out of it. You can be the judge. Sue, you know that he's going to ride Jerico tomorrow?"

"Of course."

"Which isn't a very peaceful thing for a man about to be married to do. Anyway, he's going to ride Jerico. But do you know what horse he's betting on?"

"No."

"On Long Tom."

"But . . . I don't understand. He's riding Jerico."

"He is."

"And surely no horse can beat Jerico. Everyone says no horse around here can beat Jerico."

"And maybe they're right."

"Then why should Jim bet on another horse?"

"Because he's riding Jerico."

"My brain is whirling, Garry. What does it mean?"

"You understand that everyone who bets against Jerico will get long odds . . . five dollars for one?"

"I've heard that."

"Doesn't Jim need money?"

"I think so."

"Then don't you see? He's betting on Long Tom because he's going to see to it that Jerico won't win the race."

"You mean he won't give Jerico an honest ride?"

"Just that."

He thought that the silence that followed would never end.

Then she said: "It isn't possible."

"I've brought you the proof."

He placed the sack of money on her knees, lighted a match, and by that light spread out Jim Orchard's note for her to read. Of course she would know the handwriting. And she did know it. She suddenly sank back into the chair, and Garry Munn removed both money and paper.

"I'm sorry, Sue," he said, after a proper interval.

No answer.

"It isn't a pleasant thing to do, but you see the

boat I'm in? I ask you, friend to friend, could I let you go on with a man like Jim Orchard . . . a man who would even cheat a horse?"

"I understand."

"You don't hold it against me?"

"No."

For some reason he would have preferred it if she had broken into tears. This thin whisper spoke of a heart withering with pain.

"Once more I'm sorry, Sue . . . and good night."

"Good night, Garry."

And that was all.

But Garry knew well enough that no matter how honestly Jim Orchard rode the next day, if Jerico lost the race Jim had lost Sue Hampton.

XI

It should have been a very quiet and unimportant affair, that race of the next day, because there was a horse entered whose appearance seemed to remove all hope of competition. In spite of the fact that Jerico was entered, several of the cattlemen had decided to let their horses run, but that was merely because they were good sports, and not because they had any hope of beating the black stallion. Garrison had put in his Foxy; Oldham had entered Snorter; Lewis had Trix; and Noonan was backing Mame; to say nothing of

Long Tom, the stranger. But it was felt that these horses were merely a background against which Jerico would appear the more glorious.

There were two elements, however, which gave the race a touch of the spectacular. In the first place one could never tell if the mustang would run quietly from the beginning to the end. There seemed every possibility that Jim Orchard had mastered the strange horse, but that remained to be seen. He was as apt as not to stop in the middle of the race and buck like a devil. The second exciting element was that a head as cool as that of Garry Munn had actually chosen to bet against Jerico.

A little money would not have made a great deal of difference, but Garry was apparently willing to stake his entire fortune. It became known that he had stretched his credit at the bank to the uttermost limit to supply the cash and, when that cash was gone, he was willing to give his note for any amount. At first the cattlemen held back, suspecting a trick. After they had gone down to see Jerico out for an exercise canter with Jim Orchard in the saddle, acting like a docile old family pet under the hand of the cowpuncher, and when, again, they had seen Tim Hogan trotting Long Tom at a shuffling, far-stepping gait, they decided that a temporary insanity had taken possession of the young rancher, and they began to cover his money in great chunks. Bets began to be registered in sums of a thousand up. Under the hammering of Garry Munn's fortune the odds dropped slowly from ten to one to two to one.

The cattlemen were as sure that Jerico would win as they were that they walked and breathed, but the confidence of Garry, backed by money, made them more conservative as the hour for the race approached. Yet two to one was fat enough, when a man was betting on a sure thing, and Garry Munn kept pouring out his fortune in money and notes, until the very value of his ranch itself was almost represented in his outstanding promises.

In spite of that it was the happiest morning of Munn's life. He went to the race track as if he were stepping into a gold mine.

A full mile around, the track had been hastily constructed and roughly leveled. A flimsy fence on either side of the roadway directed the horses and riders. There was no pretense at a stand to hold the crowd. Both inside and outside the oval track the throng stood along the fences or sat in their buckboards or in the saddle to look over the heads of the early comers. But the noise of wagering was confined to one moving spot, and that was where Garry Munn walked. He paused near Sue Hampton. She stood close to the fence, both hands resting on the top of the post, as though she needed that support. When he spoke to her, she returned no answer. Indeed, her face was that of a sleepwalker. It troubled even the cold nerve of Garry Munn as he turned away.

But, after all, he argued to himself, *Jim's as big a crook as I am . . . almost. What's to choose between us except that he's a beggar, and I'll be rich before tonight?*

His smile returned, and his voice rang as gaily as ever, shouting: "My last thousand, gentlemen! Who'll cover it? One to two on Long Tom. There he goes. How do you like his looks? I'm betting on those long legs. Two jumps and he'll be around the track. Who takes me up?"

The ring of that familiar voice struck across to Jim Orchard as he stood beside the head of Jerico. Tom, the old Negro, was close by.

"You see them others?" he said, pointing to the cattle ponies that were being trotted up and down to make sure they would be warm and loose-muscled for the race. "Them boys thinks they's on horses, but they ain't. There's only one horse here, and that's Jerico. Oh, Jerry'll show 'em what's what today!"

Jim Orchard returned no answer. He had seen close to the fence the white face of Sue Hampton, and the ugly thought had come to him: *How is it possible for me to win the woman I most love and honor in the world by a piece of mean chicanery? How will it be possible for me to face her level eyes after this race?*

He turned for consolation to Jerico himself. The great stallion kept always behind his new rider, as though he wanted protection from the crowd, which he hated. If a man passed too close to him, his ears flattened instantly, and his nostrils expanded and quivered, but, as soon as the shadow of fear had passed, he would touch the shoulder of Jim Orchard with his nose and then meet the glance of the rider with pricking ears. It was as though he said in mute language: *I understand. You look the same, but you're different.*

Every time Jim Orchard saw that noble head his heart sank.

Long Tom came onto the track and was greeted by a murmur of mingled interest and amusement. They were not used to seeing such horses as this, these cattlemen. They could not understand how those gaunt muscles, flattening and sinking at shoulders and thighs, might mean elastic striding power and astonishing speed. To them he was more a freak than a horse for riding.

But Jim Orchard had seen the bay in action, and he understood. It comforted him to see Long Tom. No matter how he rode, what chance had Jerico against this speed machine?

Now they were summoning the horses to the post. He mounted Jerico and jogged slowly to the position. Opposite Sue Hampton, in spite of Jerico's plunging, as they approached the fence and the crowd, he cut far in and leaned to speak to her.

"Give Jerico luck, Sue!" he called.

She raised her white face and murmured an answer. It was not until he had passed on that he straightened out the meaning of the words.

"Oh, Jim, I'm praying for you."

Why for me?

He had no time to get to the meaning of the riddle. He was coming past the main section of the crowd, where they were packed around the line that was both start and finish. What a roar went up to greet the black! Jerico crouched and quivered before it. Then, as though he understood that this was a welcome and not a threat, he tossed up his head proudly and looked across the mass of faces.

The places were tossed for. Foxy got the inside; Snorter was number two; then came Jerico with an ample space on either side for fear of his heels; then Trix, then Mame, and last of all, on the outside, was Long Tom.

"There's your luck. There's the end of your freak horse, Garry!" shouted someone in the crowd.

The voice was hissed. It was thought a shameful thing to laugh at a man who had wagered the very home over his head on a horse race. Betting on such a scale was a thing to be almost reverenced.

Jerico behaved at the post as though he had

raced a hundred times, standing perfectly still, with the calming voice of Jim Orchard to steady him. Jim looked across the line of horses and saw little Tim Hogan bouncing up and down, as Long Tom pranced awkwardly, eager to be away.

A voice came to him from a distance. It was Judge McCreavy giving the riders their instructions and telling them not to swing wide at the turns, for fear of cutting off horses behind them. He added other instructions. There was a pause. The crowd became deadly silent, and then the crack of the pistol.

The others were off their marks in a flash, but Jim Orchard purposely allowed Jerico to twist his head around at the last moment. When he twitched the head around and straightened Jerico to run after the pack, there was a groan from the crowd—the rest of the horses were lengths and lengths away! Jim Orchard, calmly, bitterly, cast his eye over that straining line of horseflesh ahead, with the riders bending low over their necks. Each was laboring to the full speed— each except Long Tom. The gaunt bay galloped clumsily, slowly, slowly, on the outside of the string—and yet, somehow, he floated along abreast of the best of the others, and a yell of wonder came from the crowd.

Jim Orchard understood and swallowed a smile. Tim Hogan must have been instructed to make this seem as much like a race as possible,

He would race Long Tom along with the rest of the pack, until they straightened away around the last turn with the finish in sight.

Suddenly all things were blotted from the mind of Jim except the one miraculous fact that the horses, which raced ahead of him, were coming back to Jerico as if they were walking, and he running at full speed. Running, indeed!

The evening before, for a hundred yards or so, he had loosed Jerico down the open road and had thought the gait of the stallion breathtaking, but that was nothing compared to the way the black was running now. His body seemed to settle more and more to the ground as his stride lengthened. His ears were blown back flat against his neck. He poured himself over the track. Run? Jim Orchard had never dreamed that horseflesh could race with such smooth, machine-like strides, never a jolt up and down, but driving always straight ahead with dizzy speed.

There was no question that Jerico understood that this was a race, and that he loved it. As for the riders on the other horses, he did not appear to think of them. All that he knew was that here was an old custom of the free days, when the wild band of horses had raced for the water hole. And in the old days his place had always been in the front, leading the rest. He hated this rear running. Snorting the dust out of his nostrils, he sprang on at a harder pace.

Each furlong was marked by a white post and, as the signal for the first eighth flashed by him, Orchard found himself on the very heels of the pack. He drew back on the reins with an iron hand. There was not the slightest response. Jerico had the bit securely in his teeth.

Would the black devil run away and make him break that contract with Tim Hogan? He leaned desperately and called gently to Jerico, and suddenly the head was raised, the ears pricked, and from his running gait the stallion broke into a great rocking gallop. Yet even that pace held him up with the others.

In the distance Jim heard the crowd yelling its delight. That first burst of Jerico's speed meant everything to them. They would expect him to go on now, and leave the others trailing behind them.

He swung Jerico to the right and drove him straight into a pocket! Trix and Mame ran to left and right of him, and Long Tom and Foxy were in front. The crowd shouted: "Dirty work! They're boxing Jerico! Let him through!"

They called to each of the other riders in turn, berating them, but the wedge-like formation held, and Jerico galloped easily, easily in the rear.

XII

He could only pray that that pocket formation would hold. They were yelling advice to him to draw back and ride around the others, but he stuck doggedly in his place. To Jerico it was a manifest torment. Again and again he came up against the bit, and then tossed his head impatiently as he heard the steady voice of the master calling him back. Plainly the heart of the stallion was breaking. His place was in front, with the sweet, clean air in his nostrils, not back there breathing the dust of all these horses.

Jim Orchard heard a shrill, cracked cry above the rest. He looked across the track and saw old Tom standing beside the track with old Glory, terrified by the noise, trying to wedge his way to a place of safety between the legs of the Negro.

When they reached the turn at the first quarter, the pocket opened as the horses swung wide around the turn, and a clear way opened before Jerico. He would have sprung through like a greyhound, but the voice of the rider called him back. Then Jim Orchard heard a cry of dismay from the crowd and, looking ahead, he saw the reason for it. Tim Hogan had apparently decided that he had waited long enough and now he was out to show the rubes what real speed in horseflesh meant.

Long Tom had thrust out his long neck, and now he was driving away from the rest. In vain they flogged and yelled at their mounts—Long Tom still drew away, and the crowd groaned.

For one thing Jim was glad; it was no longer necessary to disguise the speed of Jerico. There went Long Tom full tilt. He could loose the black and let him do his best with his sixty-pound handicap. The gap was still opened before him and now, touching the flank of the stallion with his open hand, he sent Jerico through it. It was a marvelous thing, that response from the black. Foxy and Trix drifted back to him and then disappeared behind his shoulders, their heads jerking foolishly up and down as they strove in vain to meet that terrific pace.

But Jerico had slipped through, and there was only Long Tom racing ahead. The three-furlong pole whipped past in a flash of white.

"Oh, Jerry, boy," said Orchard. "You ain't got a chance. If we had that skinny bay in the open country, we'd make a fool of him inside half an hour. Go it, boy, but there's not a chance."

He dropped his head and waited—waited for Jerico to slacken and fall back under that grilling strain. But there was no slackening. Instead there was a perceptible increase in the rush of wind that beat down the brim of his sombrero.

The groaning of the crowd had ceased, followed by a prolonged series of wild, cowboy yells. Jim looked up again and to his astonishment he saw that Long Tom had not increased his lead. Was Tim Hogan keeping the bay back?

No, Tim Hogan rode with his tiny body flattened along Tom's neck, giving his mount his head, and Long Tom was doing his noble best. But that best was not good enough!

The stunning truth came home to Jim Orchard. In spite of the cruel handicap of weight, in spite of the poor start, Jerico was slowly, surely, methodically cutting down the lead. Indeed, it might be that the very slowness of the start and the delay while he was held in the pocket were helping him now. It might be that early handicap and restraint had allowed the great stallion to come slowly into his pace, warming him for the greater test, sharpening his nerves and rousing his mighty heart.

All that heart, beyond a doubt, was going into the race for supremacy. By the quiver of the strong body beneath him, Jim knew that the stallion was giving his best. He spoke again, and slowly, unwillingly, tossing his head as though to ask for an explanation, Jerico answered the call and slackened his pace.

But Tim Hogan had been frightened. Jim saw the little fellow glance back and then draw his whip. Long Tom shot into a great lead at once, and there was the long, despairing murmur from the crowd.

The half-mile post gleamed and was gone behind them.

But, oddly enough, a picture came into the mind of Jim Orchard, of old Glory, the bull terrier, crowding close to the Negro for protection. Once that dog might have been among other dogs what Jerico was among other horses. One beating had robbed him of his spirit. One beating had made him what he was today, broken, skulking, a creature that made even the spirit of a man cringe with shame to see. And might not one beating do the same for Jerico? To be conquered by one of his kind, under the handicap that men had imposed on him, might well break his heart. And what would Jerico be then? A stumbling, worthless, shameful caricature of the horse he was today. Whose work? The work of Jim Orchard!

Still keeping the rein taut, he looked ahead. Long Tom had opened up a great gap, and the five-furlong post darted like a ghost behind them! Seeking for courage, Jim Orchard looked back where the crowd was packed at the finish. It was a white blur of faces, and somewhere among them was the face of the girl praying for him— for Jim Orchard. Underneath him Jerico was straining to be free from the restraint, praying, if ever a horse could pray, to follow Long Tom

211

with every ounce of energy in his glorious body.

It was already hopeless to overtake Tim Hogan, surely. And besides, there was the girl—but logic had no hold on Jim Orchard. Suddenly he had dashed the hat from his head with a yell that went pealing across the track and thrilled the crowd. It caught the ear of Tim Hogan and made him turn again in the saddle to look back. It caught Jerico as if with a new force and shot him forward at full speed.

Jim was riding for victory—victory for Jerico, and wretched defeat for himself. But the latter seemed nothing. His fortune—Sue Hampton— nothing mattered except that Jerico should have an honest chance to win his race. A weight fell from his heart as he made that resolve, and it seemed as though a literal weight fell from the back of Jerico as lightly he sprang forward.

Tim Hogan had taken warning. His whip was out again, and he turned the last corner and drove the tall bay frantically into the homestretch. Jim Orchard swung forward in the stirrups, throwing his weight across the withers, where weight least burdens a racing horse.

"Jerico," he whispered, "give all you've got. It may be enough. It's got to be enough. Go after 'em. Go after 'em."

It had seemed impossible for the stallion to gain another particle of speed, and yet there was a perceptible response now. He streaked around the turn. The three-quarters post gleamed and fled behind them, and the shout of the crowd at the finish crashed up the track and thundered in the ears of Orchard.

The bit was no longer in the teeth of Jerico. He had loosed his grip as though he felt that there could be no danger in the guidance of this rider. He had surrendered himself to the will of a master as though he knew that will would lift him on to overtake the flying bay.

The eager eye of Jim Orchard saw the distance between them diminish. Long Tom was still running nobly, but he was not ready for such a test as this. His strength was failing and Jerico, like a creature possessed with a devil, seemed to gain with every stride he made. Well did the rider know the secret of that strength. It was the strength which men use in lost causes and forlorn hopes; it was the generous last effort of the fighter.

Now he heard Tim Hogan cursing—a shrill voice that piped back at him, the words cut short and blown away by the wind of the mad gallop. And then the yelling of the crowd drowned all other sound.

One name on all those lips. It roared and beat into the very soul of Orchard. One name all those frantic hands were imploring: "Jerico! Jerico! Jerico!"

Tim Hogan glanced back for the third time,

and Jim Orchard caught a glimpse of a white, convulsed face. Then the jockey whirled and was back at his work, lifting Long Tom ahead with savage slashes of the whip.

The seven-furlong post shot past. The finish lay straight ahead. Two breaths and the race would be over!

The cry of the mob became Orchard's cry in the ear of the straining stallion: "Jerico! Jerico!" Every time there was a quiver of the thin ears that flattened against the stallion's neck.

Now they were on the hip of Long Tom, and the tail, flying straight back with the wind of the gallop, was blowing beside Jim Orchard's stirrup.

"Jerico! Jerico!"

For every call there was an effort like the efforts which answered the whip of Tim Hogan! Orchard felt that his voice had become a power. It was pouring an electric energy out of his body, and out of his soul into the body and soul of his horse. It lifted him past the hip of Long Tom; it brought the black nose to the flank of the bay—the flank so gaunt and hollow with the strain of the gallop. It carried him to the saddle girth.

Too late, for the massed faces at the finish line were straight before them. "Jerico!"

Oh, great heart, what an answer! The scream of Tim Hogan and the sting of his whip brought no such response as this. Foam spattered the breast of Long Tom, and still he labored, still he winced under the whip, but his speed was slackening, his head was going up, up—the head of a beaten horse. Beaten he was in spirit, whether he won or lost.

Would he win? There was Judge McCreavy standing at the finish post with his arm extended, as though to point out to them that this was the end.

"Jerico!"

Past the girth and to the shoulder with one lunge.

"Jerico!"

And now only the snaky head of the bay is in the lead.

"Jerico!"

They are over the finish. The shout of the mob was a scream and a sob in one.

But who had conquered? There stood Long Tom, with dropped head, and here was Jerico, dancing beneath him, as he drew to a halt and then turned and faced the crowd with his glorious head raised. He waited like a gladiator for their judgment, and with what a voice they gave it, all in a chorus, thundering in waves around Jim Orchard.

"Jerico!"

Jerico had won. After that, all things grew hazy before the staring eyes of Jim Orchard. He was searching in that crowd for one face.

He saw Tim Hogan slowly dismounting. He

saw Garry Munn standing like one who has been stunned. And then she came to him through the mob. For all their excitement, they gave way before her as though they knew it was her right.

Here was old Tom with the terrible head of Jerico in his fearless arms, weeping like a child.

Here was Sue Hampton holding up both her hands to him, with a face that opened heaven to Jim Orchard.

"Jerico's won," he said miserably, "but I've lost . . . everything."

"But nothing matters . . . don't you see? . . . except . . ."

She was sobbing, in her excitement, so that she could scarcely speak.

"Except what, Sue?"

"Except that Jerico has won, Jim . . . for you and for me."

SUNSET WINS

I

His father was a Macdonald of the old strain which once claimed the proud title of Lord of the Isles. His mother was a Connell of that family which had once owned Connell Castle. After that terrible slaughter of the Connells at the Boyne, those who were left of the race fled to the colonies. After the Macdonalds had followed Bonny Prince Charlie into England in that luckless year, 1715, the remnants of the proscribed race waited for vengeance among the Highlands, or else followed the Connells across the Atlantic.

The Connells were great black men, with hands that could crush flagons or break heads. The Macdonalds were red-headed giants, with heaven-blue eyes and a hunger for battle. But the passing of generations changed them. They became city dwellers, in part, and those who dwelt in cities shrank in stature and diminished in numbers. They became merchants, shrewd dealers, capable of sharp practice. They lived by their wits and not by the strength of their hands. They gave corporals and raw-handed sergeants to the war of the Revolution, and to the Civil War, nearly four generations later, they gave majors and colonels and generals. Their minds were growing and their bodies were shrinking.

And so at last a Mary Connell, small, slim-throated, silken black of hair, wedded a Gordon Macdonald, with shadowy red hair and mild, patient, blue eyes. They were little people. He was a scant five feet and six inches in height, and yet he seemed big and burly when he stood by the side of his wife. What manner of children should they have? For five years there was no child at all, and then Mary died giving birth to a son. He was born shrieking rage at the world, with his red hands doubled into fat balls of flesh, and his blue eyes staring up with the battle fury—he was born with red hair gleaming upon his head. His father looked down upon him in sadness and bewilderment. Surely this was no true son of his!

His wonder grew with the years. At thirteen, young Gordon Macdonald was taller than his father and heavier. He had great, long-fingered bony hands and huge wrists, from the latter of which the tendons stood out, as though begging for the muscles that were to come. And his joy was not in his books and his tutor. His pleasure was in the streets. When the door was locked upon him, he stole out of his bed at night and climbed down from the window of his room, like a young pirate, and went abroad in search of adventure. And he would come back again two days later with his clothes in rags, his face purpled and swollen with blows, and his knuckles raw. They sent him to a school famous for Latin and broken heads. He prostrated two masters within three months with nervous breakdowns, and he was expelled from the school weak, bruised, but triumphant.

"Force is the thing for him then," said his weary-minded parent. "Let us discipline his body and pray God that time may bring him mildness. Labor was the curse laid on Adam. Let his shoulders now feel its weight."

So he was made an apprentice in a factory, at the ripe age of fifteen, to bow his six feet two of bones and sinews with heavy weights of iron and to callous his hands with the rough handles of sledge-hammers. But though he came home at night staggering, he came home singing. And if he grew lean with the anguish of labor in the first month, he began to grow fat on it in the second. His father cut off his allowance. But on Saturday nights Gordon began to disappear. Money rolled into his pockets, and he dressed like a dandy. Presently his father read in one paper of a rising young light heavyweight who was crushing old and experienced pugilists in the first and second rounds under the weight of a wild-cat onslaught. In a second paper he saw a picture of this Red Jack and discovered that he was his one and only son!

After that he took his head between his hands

and prayed for guidance, and he received an inspiration to send his boy away from the wiles of the wicked city for a year and a day. So he signed Gordon Macdonald on a sailing ship bound for Australia. He bade his boy farewell, gave him a blessing, and died the next month, his mind shattered by a financial crash. But he had accomplished one thing at least with his son— Gordon Macdonald came back to Manhattan no more.

In the port of Sydney, far from his homeland, he celebrated his seventeenth birthday with a drunken carousal, and the next day he insulted the first mate, broke his jaw with a pile-driving jab, and was thrown into the hold in irons. He filed through his chains that night, went above, threw the watch into the sea, dived in after him, and swam ashore.

He was hotly pursued by the infuriated captain. The police were appealed to. He stole a horse to help him on his flight. He was cornered at the end of the seventh day, starved, but lion-like. With his bare hands he attacked six armed men. He smashed two ribs of one, the jaw of another, and fractured the skull of the third before he was brought down spouting crimson from a dozen bullet wounds.

The nursing he received was not tender, but he recovered with a speed that dazed the doctor. Then he was promptly clapped into prison for resisting arrest, for theft, and for assaulting the officers of the law.

For three months he poured upon the cross-section of the world of crime that was presented to him in a wide, thick slab in the prison. Then, when he was weary of being immersed in the shadows of the world, he knocked down a guard, climbed a wall, tore a rifle from the hands of another guard, and stunned the fellow with a blow across the head, sprang down on the farther side, dodged away through a fusillade of bullets, reached the desert land, lived there like a hunted beast for six months, with a horse for a companion, a rifle for a wife, and a revolver for a chosen friend. At last he reached a seaport and took ship again on the free blue waters.

When the ship touched at Bombay, the hand of the law seized him again. He broke away the next night, reached the Himalayas after three months of wild adventure, plunged into the wastes of Tibet, joined a caravan that carried him into central Asia, came to St. Petersburg a year later, shipped to Brazil, rounded the Horn on a tramp freighter, and deserted at a Mexican port.

At the age of nineteen he rode across the border into Texas for the first time. He stood six feet two and a half inches in his bare feet. He weighed two hundred pounds stripped to the buff. He knew guns and fighting tricks, as a saint knows the Bible, and his whole soul ached every day to find some man or men capable of giving him battle that would exercise him to the uttermost of his gigantic strength.

But on his long pilgrimage he had learned a great truth: no matter how a man defies his fellows, he must not defy the law. For the law reaches ten thousand miles as easily as a man reaches across the table for a glass of water. And no matter if a man has a hand of iron, the law has fingers of steel.

Suppose the mind of a fox planted in the body of a Bengal tiger, a beast of royal power and a brain of devilish cunning. Such was Gordon Macdonald. He looked like a lion, he thought like a fox, and he fought like ten devils, shoulder to shoulder.

First he joined the Rangers, not for the glory of suppressing crime, but for the glory of the dangers to be dared in that wild service. He gained ten commendations in as many months for fearless work, but in the eleventh month he was requested to resign. The Texas Rangers prefer to capture living criminals rather than dead ones.

So Gordon Macdonald resigned and rode again on his friendless way. He rode for ten years through a thousand adventures, and in ten years no man's eyes lighted to see him come, no woman smiled when he was near her, no child laughed and took his hand. The very dogs snarled at him and shrank from his path. But Macdonald cared for none of these things. The spirit that rides on a thunderbolt does not hope for applause from the world it is about to strike. No more cared Red Macdonald. For he was tinglingly awake to one thing only, and that was the hope of battle. Speed, such as hides in the wrist of a cat, strength, such as waits in the paw of a grizzly, wisdom, such as lingers in the soul of a wolf— these were his treasures. Through all the years he fought his battles in such a way that the lie was first given to him by the other man, and the other man first drew his gun. Therefore the law passed him by unscathed. And all the years he followed, with a sort of rapturous intentness, a ghost of hope that someday he would meet a man who would be his equal, some giant of force, with the speed of a curling whiplash and the malignity of a demon. Someday he would come on the trail of a great devastator, an incarnate spirit of evil, and these men who now ceased talking and eyed him askance when he entered a room, these women who grew pale as he passed, would come to him and fall on their knees and beg him to spare them. He carried that thought always in his heart of hearts, like a secret comfort.

Such was Gordon Macdonald at the age of thirty. He was as striking in face as in his big body. That arched and cruel nose, that long stern chin, that fiery hair, uncombable on his head, and, above all, his blue eyes stopped the thoughts and hearts of men. One felt the endless stirring impulse in him. To look in his eyes was like looking on the swift changes of color that run down the cooling iron toward the point. It was impossible to imagine this man sleeping. It was impossible to conceive of this man for an instant inactive of mind, for he seemed to be created to forge wily schemes and plan cruel deeds.

He had crowded the events of a dozen ordinary lives into his short span of years. And still, insatiable of action, he kept on the trail which has only one ending. One might have judged that with such a career behind him, some of it would have been written in his face, but even in this he was deceptive. To be sure, when he frowned, a thousand lines and shadows appeared in his face—he might have been taken for a man of forty. But when he threw back his head and laughed—laughed with a savage satisfaction for work accomplished, or for danger in the prospect, he looked no more than a wild youth of twenty.

Such was Macdonald in his thirtieth year. Such was Macdonald when he saw Sunset, and at once he sensed that the fates had arranged the encounter.

II

The horse had his name from his color. When the brilliant colors at the end of the day begin to fade from the clouds, and when they are only shimmering with a rusty red, such was the tint of the hide of the horse, and yet the mane and tail and the four stockings of the stallion were jet black. It was that rich, strange color that first startled Macdonald and held his mind. It was like the thick blood with light striking across it, he thought, and that grim simile stayed in his mind.

The thought struck an echo through his brain at once. There was something of fate in this meeting, he felt. A strange surety grew up in him that his destiny was inextricably entangled with Sunset. An equal surety came to him that that destiny was a gloomy thing. If he had that horse, evil would come of it, and yet the horse he must have.

He rode closer to the edge of the corral and examined the stallion more in detail. It was not color alone in which Sunset was glorious. He was one of those rare freaks of horseflesh in which size is combined with an exquisite proportion and fine working of details. It is rare to find a tall man who is not poorly put together, whose legs are not too long, or whose arms are not too lean;

there are sure to be flaws and weaknesses when a man stands over six feet in height. And, rare as it is to find a big man who conforms to the Greek canons, it is rarer still to find a tall horse neither too long nor too short coupled with bone to support his bulk, but not lumpy and heavy in the joints, with a straight, strong back, with a neck neither too heavy nor too long and gaunt to balance comfortably a head that is apt to be as big as the head of a cart horse, or as ludicrously small as the head of a pony.

Sunset avoided all these possible defects. One knew at a glance that he would fit the standard. So exact, indeed, were his proportions that it might have seemed with the first survey that he was too lean and gangling of legs, but, when one drew closer and gave more professional attention to his survey, one noted the great depth of body where the girth ran, the wide, square quarters, rich in driving power, the flat and ample bone, the round hoofs, black as ink, the powerful sweep of the long shoulders, dimpled over and rippling with muscles like the tangled lashes of a thousand whips. He stood a scant inch under seventeen hands, but he was made with the scrupulous exactness of a fifteen-hand thoroughbred, one of those incredible carvings of Nature that dance like little kings and queens about the turf at a horse show, or take the jumps as though winged with fire.

And here were the same things drawn to scale and made gigantic. The great heart of Macdonald contracted with yearning. He looked down with unspeakable disgust to the nag that bore him. Big-headed, long-eared, squat and shapeless of build, the gelding had only one commendable quality, and that was an immense strength which was capable of supporting even the solid bulk of Macdonald, with a jog trot that might last from morning to night. But on such a steed he was a veritable slave. If he offended, a swift-riding posse might swoop down and overtake him in a half hour's run. No wonder that he did not violate the law when he was damned by slowness of movement. And what availed him all his prowess, if he could neither pursue nor flee? Were there not a score of men who had insulted him and then avoided the inevitable lightning flash of his revenge by springing upon the backs of neat-footed horses and darting away across the mountains?

He looked up to the ragged sides of those mountains. The rider of such a horse as Sunset could make his home among those peaks. From those impracticable heights he could sweep down like a hawk on the wing and take toll from the groveling men of the plains—strike—ravage—destroy—beat down enemies—award justice for past injuries—and then away on wings again—wings strong enough to sweep him up the slopes and back to safety, while the sweating posse labored and puffed and cursed and moiled vainly in the dust far behind him.

No wonder that Macdonald looked back from those distant heights to the stallion with a heart on fire with eagerness. The speed of an eagle, the strength of a lion, and the heart of a lamb. Yonder stood the giant horse nosing the hand of the man who was talking softly to him and stroking his sleek neck. Macdonald dismounted. He stepped closer to the pair.

He had one gracious quality, and that was a soft and deep bass voice. He used it with more effect because in all his travels he had picked up no slang. He spoke the same pure tongue that he had learned in his boyhood.

"I wonder," he said to the stranger, "if you're the man who owns this horse?"

"Sunset?" The other turned, as though surprised that anyone should have asked such a question. He was a tall and slenderly-built youth, with long tawny hair, a brown, weather-marked face with joyous gray eyes looking out at Macdonald. "Yep," he said. "I own Sunset."

"Sunset?" echoed Macdonald, and he looked back to the stallion. It was an appropriate name, and he said so. It was doubly appropriate now, as the big horse turned, and a wave of red light rippled along his flank, like a highlight traveling over bright silk.

At the deep and quiet sound of his voice, Sunset came closer, snorted softly his suspicion, then reached out with bright and mischievous eyes and nibbled at the brown back of Macdonald's hand.

"Oh, he doesn't seem to be afraid, does he?" asked Macdonald of his companion in the profoundest wonder.

"Why should he be afraid?" asked the other, frowning. "He's been raised right and treated right. He don't connect with gents with clubs and spurs, like most of the horses around these here parts."

Macdonald looked over his shoulder, and his gelding flattened its ears and stared at the master with concentrated malice. Back to Sunset turned Gordon Macdonald. The teeth of the stallion had caught up a fold of skin on the back of his hand and pinched it very gently. Yet, as though he had committed a crime deserving punishment, the red horse started away, tossing and shaking his head. No rough curses followed him. He came back again slowly. Once more he sniffed at the stranger. Once more he came back and thrust out his beautiful head. Wonder of wonders, he permitted that great, strong hand of Macdonald to reach and touch his velvet muzzle. He permitted the tips of those terrible fingers to rub his forehead, to touch his silken ears, to stray along his throat. Nay, he grew so emboldened that he reached high. He caught the brim of Macdonald's hat. He twitched it off, and then, wheeling like a dog playing a game, half afraid and half delighted, he bolted across the field, whipping the hat from side to side and flashing his heels in the air.

"Hey!" yelled the owner. "Come back here, Sunset! Say, stranger, I'm mighty sorry that happened . . . looks like a good hat, too."

He broke off in his apologies. Fifty dollars in gold had been paid the Mexican who first owned that sombrero. But now Macdonald was staring after a fleeing horse, like one enchanted by a dream of beauty. The long sweep of that gallop made him dizzy with delight. His stern lips parted to the tenderest of smiles. On the farther side of the field Sunset dropped the sombrero and dashed his hoofs upon it. In an instant it was a mass of rents and fragments. And behold, Macdonald turned to his companion a laughing face.

"He's like a big, happy dog," he said.

The other stared upon him with no less surprise than if he had been convicted that instant of lunacy. And, indeed, there was something wild in this careless throwing away of a sombrero, dearer to a cowpuncher's heart than aught except his gun.

After the episode, Sunset picked up the hat again and came back at full gallop, the fragments dangling from his teeth, his head thrust out, his ears flattened, his mane flying like the plumes above a Grecian helmet, swift as an arrow loosed from the string, the ground shivering under the impact of his beating hoofs. A red flash of danger he shot at them, then threw himself back and slid to a halt on stiffly braced legs, while his hoofs plowed up long strips of the turf. At the very feet of Macdonald he dropped the hat.

"Like he expected a lump of sugar for spoiling my hat," Macdonald said, and laughed again. "And look at this! He comes right back to my hand again. Man, man, there's only one horse in the world . . . only one horse in the world."

"Come here, Sunset," said the master. "Come here, I say."

But Sunset only wavered toward his owner. Then he returned to the fascinating task of trying to catch a lock of Macdonald's fire red hair in his teeth. What it meant to Macdonald no man could know. Perhaps a mother feeling the tugging hands of an infant could understand how his heart ached with joy to see this magnificent dumb creature defy him without malice and tease him as though he were some harmless child.

"What have you done to Sunset?" growled the young owner. "Never saw him act up like that to any other man."

It was wine of purest delight to Macdonald.

"He doesn't take up with strangers, you say?" he asked greedily.

"Takes them with his heels, if he can."

"Well," said Macdonald, "he's no common horse. He understands. He understands, eh, old boy?" He turned abruptly on the youth. "What's your name?"

"Rory Moore."

"Moore, is your horse for sale?"

"Nope."

"Moore, I've got five hundred dollars in my pocket."

"He's not for sale. Why, I raised him."

"Look here, five hundred is quite a lot. It takes a long time for a cowpuncher to save that much." He put the amount in Moore's hand.

"No use talking, stranger," declared Moore.

"Six hundred, then."

"Not if you made it six thousand."

"Moore, here's nine hundred and eighty dollars. It's yours. Give me the horse!"

"Not for nine thousand eight hundred."

Moore recoiled a little, for the expression of Macdonald had changed. His lips had stiffened. His big body had trembled. There was even a change in the hand that had been stroking the neck of the stallion, for the horse suddenly drew back and sniffed suspiciously at the bony fingers. But if there had been a glimpse of danger in the face of Macdonald, he smoothed it away quickly enough and managed to smile.

"No way in the world that you'd give up that horse . . . couldn't be taken from you?"

"Not unless the luck was against me."

"Luck?"

"I mean I've never backed down at dice for any man. And, in fact," Rory Moore was laughing at the thought, "I'd stake my life on my luck. Look here, I've got a pair of dice with me. Your nine hundred against Sunset . . . one roll."

Eagerly Macdonald reached for the little cubes, then drew his hand back with a groan. "I never gamble," he said.

"What?" cried the other, as though the sun had vanished from the heavens. "Never gamble?"

"No." He turned, took one last, long look at Sunset, who had pressed his breast against the fence, as though eager to follow, and then stepped to his gelding.

"What name'll I remember you by?" asked Moore.

But Macdonald did not seem to hear. He had thrown himself into the saddle and spurred the gelding down the road toward town, whose roofs already pushed up above the trees.

III

"But how a gold digger like you," Macdonald said, "could ever go broke, I don't see. You can make the cards do everything but talk, can't you? And I've watched you practice with the dice and call your throw nine times out of ten, even bouncing them against a wall."

The gambler lifted his wan, lean face from his hands. Then he shrugged his shoulders.

"Yep," he said, "I can do that. And I had my big game planted, Macdonald. There was a fortune in sight . . . a hundred thousand, if there was a cent in that game. I had the cards stacked. Nothing better. Gent started betting against me. He had two aces and two jacks. My guns, how well I remember! I'd given him the ace of spades and the ace of hearts and the jack of spades and the jack of diamonds. He opened on the jacks, and I gave him the aces on the draw. The fifth card ought to have been the seven of clubs. I had three little deuces, but they looked big against two pair. I figured him to be bluffing. He began to raise. I raised him right back. He began to sweat. I figured that he was sorry for his bluff but thought that he could work it out. He saw me and raised me right back.

"Then I smeared in the rest of my chips . . . every cent I had was on that table . . . and he called. I showed my three deuces . . . I was reaching for the pot, and he laughed and put down two jacks and *three* aces on top of them. Yes, sir, it wasn't the seven of clubs that I'd given him . . . the first mistake I'd made in a hundred deals, and how I made it, I dunno. An ace full on jacks is what he hands me, and me with three measly deuces! That's how I'm busted, Macdonald."

"Just change that name, will you?" said Macdonald.

"They don't know you here?"

"No, it's new country for me."

"Me too, and bad country it is. What name do you want? I call myself Jenkins."

"Call me nothing . . . call me Red, if you wish."

"All right. And, Red, you ain't fixed to stake me, are you?"

"What?"

The gambler shrank from him with a sickly smile. "I meant to stake me to a couple of square meals, pal. I'm lined with vacancy, fact. Ain't eaten since I can remember."

Macdonald rubbed his knuckles across his chin, and under his gaze Jenkins shuddered. His eyes widened. Plainly he knew a great deal indeed about the past of this slayer of men.

"Suppose I do stake you?"

"Why, then I'll sure pay you back, partner, the minute . . ."

"Suppose I stake you to five hundred dollars?"

The jaw of Jenkins fell. "Five hundred," he whispered. "What you want of me, Mac? What can I do for you? You know I ain't any hand with a gat, or for . . ."

The raised hand of Macdonald silenced him. "I want you to gamble for me."

"Why I'd play my head off. You mean I'm to split with you after . . ."

"Shut up," said Macdonald. "I want to think."

He strode up and down the room for a time, and the rat-like, sharp eyes of Jenkins followed him guiltily back and forth. Presently he shrank back in his chair again as the bulk of the other loomed before him, and Macdonald stood still with his legs braced far apart.

"I want no split," he said. "If you win, you win, and you keep the coin you make."

Jenkins swallowed with difficulty, and his haunted eyes clung to the face of Macdonald.

"There's a youngster who lives in an old house near the town. His name is Moore."

"Oh, yes, Rory Moore."

"You know him?"

"All about him."

"What do you know?"

"The Moores used to own most of this here country. Look across the street."

Macdonald looked across to the lofty and gabled front of the hotel. It was a spacious building for such a small town, and it was set far back from the street in deep grounds, in which all the garden had perished except a scattering of shrubs.

"That used to be the Moore home," said Jenkins.

"Well?"

"Rory's father blew the whole wad of coin. He

was a hot spender. Paris was his speed, that's all. Come back with a mighty small jingle in his purse and a funny accent. The kids got his empty purse, but they couldn't inherit the funny accent." And Jenkins laughed with a malicious satisfaction. "If he wanted to throw his coin away, why wasn't poker right here in Texas as good as Monte Carlo? Down with a gent that don't patronize home folks, I say!" His thin lips writhed into a snarl of deathless malevolence.

"This youngster, Rory Moore . . . he likes to play pretty well?"

"And he usually wins. That's how he's made enough money to start his ranch. He's sure got luck with dice and cards. Well, you know what luck means."

"You mean he's crooked?"

There was an expressive shrug of the shoulders.

"I think you are lying, Jenkins."

The latter winced under the word, but he recovered himself at once.

"I ain't *seen* him crook the cards," he confessed. "But he's a bad one . . . a fighter." He stopped short, watching Macdonald, in dread lest this imputation of blame to a fighter might offend the man of battle.

But Macdonald was not thinking of himself. "He's a fighter, you say? Neat with a gun, eh?"

"Quick and certain . . . which is what counts most."

"Look here, Jenkins, would you have the nerve to sit in with Moore at a game and beat him?"

Jenkins turned white. "What if I made a slip . . . and he seen? I'd be ready for planting, right there and *pronto*!"

"What if you didn't make a slip?"

"Then I'd clean him out." He twisted his bony hands together in glee at the prospect.

"Yes, he's the sort that would bet down to his last dollar," nodded Macdonald.

"He'd bet the boots he rides in," assented Jenkins. "And if he stuck by the game, a gent could clean him out of his ranch . . . out of everything. But what's the use of talking like that? I ain't got a stake to start a game, have I?" He fixed upon Macdonald the eyes of a ferret.

"Five hundred dollars, Jenkins. I'll stake you as high as that."

"And how do we split?"

"How do you think we should?"

"I dunno," whined Jenkins. "You furnish the cash, but I take the chances. And if he thinks I'm running up the cards on him, there'll be a gun play sure."

"He has a horse . . ."

"Sunset, you mean?" asked Jenkins.

"That's the name. Jenkins, I want that horse. When you break him, he'll stake Sunset. I want Sunset, but you can keep the cash."

For a time they were both silent, the lips of

Jenkins moving, and his eyes fixed so intently upon the distance, that he reminded Macdonald of one who bet his last cent on a horse race and sees the ponies battling desperately down the homestretch.

"A man has to die sometime," Jenkins said at last. "And ain't it better to die flush than broke?"

"There's no doubt about that."

"I'll take you up, Red! Gimme that coin and I'll lay for him. I'll get him tonight. Say, Red, I been broke so long that this looks like a pile of money that you're giving me. Don't you want some sort of a receipt?"

But Macdonald, as he put the wallet back into his pocket, merely smiled. "No," he said. "I don't need a receipt."

"Sure you don't," murmured Jenkins, shivering violently, as another thought came to him. "I guess there ain't many west of the Mississippi that would try to beat you out of anything." His shivering ended in a crackling laugh. But he had a pocket bulging with money, and his spirits would not stay down. Warmth was beginning to strike through all his body.

"One thing I never could make out about you, Red," he went on.

"What's that?"

"You can do about anything that any other man can do. But you always stay shut of cards. Don't seem to want to take chances that way. But you sure made a mistake, Red. With your nerve you get by fine. The trouble with me . . . the trouble with me is that I get to thinking of what might happen, if they should find me out in a pinch, and something sort of melts in me."

It was not often that Macdonald showed any delicacy of feeling, but now he turned away to hide the scorn that darkened on his face.

"Jenkins," he said, facing the other again, "has an honest gambler a chance of winning?"

"Honest gambler!" sneered Jenkins. "There ain't any such bird."

"That's why I don't gamble," said Macdonald. "I haven't enough coin to throw away, and as for the other way of gambling, I hate a sure thing."

"But look here," argued Jenkins, "do you think that *I'm* going to play square with Rory Moore?"

Macdonald scowled upon his confederate. "I offered Moore twice the value of his horse," he explained. "He was a fool not to take it, and you're a worse fool, Jenkins, to ask questions."

IV

Here ended the talk, of course. Macdonald left Jenkins and stalked across the street to the hotel. There he went at once to his bed and flung himself upon it. Since he had not closed his eyes in forty-eight hours, he could hardly prop them open long enough to finish his bedside cigarette, peering through the shadows of the room at the old photographs and pictures that hung along the walls. These might all be members of the clan of Moore—kinsmen, relations, supporters of the old power in the days when it was really great, and when this hotel was like a castle in the midst of a principality.

Such were the thoughts that formed vaguely in the mind of Macdonald before he threw his cigarette butt through the window, turned on his side, and was instantly asleep. It was a sleep filled with visions of uncertain misery for a time, but by degrees he passed into a dream of such pleasantness that he began to smile in his sleep.

For it seemed to Macdonald that he was mounted at last upon the great red beauty, Sunset, and that he was galloping over the mountain desert like a dry leaf soaring on a wind. A dizziness of joy swept into his brain, with the sway and swing of that galloping. And there was perfect accord between the red horse and himself. A pressure of his knee was as good as a twist of the reins, and his voice was both bit and spur.

In the meantime he came to a river twisting among the hills, a swift, straight stream, save where it now and then dodged the knees of a hill and plunged on again. Macdonald looked upon that river with a careful eye, but he could not remember having seen it before.

He went on up its bank, glorying in the brown rushing of the waters with streaks and riffles of yellow foam upon the surface. On either side the banks were being gouged away. Here and there trees were toppling on the edges of the banks, with half their foothold torn away. And even the hills of rock, which the stream dodged perforce, were rudely assaulted and carved by the currents.

And, just as this dashing and thundering torrent was different from other peaceful rivers full of quiet, of pauses and starts, was not he, also, equally different from other men? Did he not bear down those who opposed him? A thousand crimes might be laid to his account, but who was strong enough or cunning enough to call him to a reckoning?

At length he came to a turn of the river, so that its main body was removed to some distance from him, as he drove on straight up the valley and, as the waters were withdrawn, it seemed to Macdonald that their voice was gathered in great, thick accents: "Turn back! Turn back! Turn back!" repeated over and over.

So startling was the clearness of that phrase that he shook his head and thundered out a fragment of a song to thrust the thought from his head, but, when he listened to the river again, it was calling as clearly as ever: "Turn back! Turn back! Turn back!"

He halted Sunset and looked about him. As he stared about him now, it seemed to Macdonald that he had indeed seen this river before. He had ridden that way, but he must have looked only casually about him. He could recall no single landmark, but he remembered the whole effect, as one remembers the sound of a human voice without being able to identify it with descriptive words.

Now he followed the stream again as it dwindled swiftly. He crossed a fork, where another creek joined it. He went on, and in another half mile he was at the big spring that gave the river birth. A little farther on he came to the divide, a ragged crest that overlooked to the east a rich plain, dotted with trees, spotted here and there with houses, and in the distance the gathered roofs of a town with a few clusters of spires above it. And, as he paused, the wind blew to him faintly the lowing of cattle made musical with distance. Another sound was forming behind him, the small voice of the creek, and again it seemed to be building words: "Turn back! Turn back! Turn back!"

Macdonald grew cold in his sleep. A heaviness of foreboding depressed him. But he reached for his guns, and they were all safe. They were all loaded. He looked again upon the plain below.

It was bright with sun, spotted with shadow as before, and all was wrapped in a misty noonday of content and prosperity.

There could be nothing to fear in this, he told himself, and straightway he gave Sunset the rein. Down the slope they went in a wild gallop. They started across the fields with Sunset jumping the fences like a bird on the wing dipping over them. And so they came suddenly to a long avenue of black walnut trees, immense and wide-spreading, trees that interlaced their branches above the head of Macdonald.

He stopped Sunset. It was more than familiar, this long double file of trees. He had seen it before. He closed his eyes. He told himself that if he turned his head he would see a section behind him, where three trees had died, and where three smaller and younger trees had been planted. He turned his head. He looked. And, behold, it was exactly as he had guessed.

It was very mysterious. He had never seen that plain before, he told himself, and yet here he was remembering an exact detail. Macdonald swallowed with difficulty. He looked hastily around him. But there was nothing to justify that warning voice that he had seemed to hear from the river among the hills. There was only the whisper of the wind among the big branches above him, and the continual shifting and inter-play of the shadows on the white road, and lazy cows, swelling with grass, had lain down in the neighboring field to chew their cuds. No, nothing could be less alarming than this, unless the rattle of approaching hoof beats bore some unsuspected danger toward him.

In a moment the rider was in view, swinging around a bend in the road. But fear? It was only a girl of eighteen or twenty on a speedy bay mare, borne backward in the saddle a little by the rate of the gallop and laughing her delight at the boughs of the walnut trees and the glimpses of the deep blue sky beyond them.

And as her face grew out upon him, Macdonald turned cold. For on the one hand he knew that he had never seen her or, at least, he had certainly never heard her voice, never heard her name, but as for her face, it was more familiar to him than his own. He had come into a ghostly land, with voices speaking from rivers and with roads on which familiar strangers journeyed,

She came straight on, and he searched her face with his stare. She was by no means like the girls he was familiar with. They rode astride like men in loosely flowing garments of khaki, but this one was clad in a tightly fitted jacket, with long tight sleeves, bunched up at the shoulders, and she was perched gracefully in a sidesaddle, with the skirt of her riding habit sweeping well down past the stirrup.

When she saw him, she threw up a hand in

greeting, and he heard her cry out in a high, sweet, tingling voice that went through and through him. The bay mare flung back and came to a halt with half a dozen stiff-legged jumps, then she busied herself touching noses with Sunset. But the girl in the sidesaddle? She had thrown her hands to Macdonald, and she was laughing, but her eyes were filled with tears.

"Oh," she cried to him, "I have been waiting so long . . . so long! I have ridden here every day for you to come, and here you are at last. I thought my heart would break with the long waiting, Gordon, but now it's breaking with happiness."

Was it from this that that voice from the river had bidden him turn back? His heart was thundering.

"Do I know you then?" he was asking her. "Have I really met you before?"

"Don't you remember?"

"I try to remember, but there's a door shut in my mind, and I can't open it."

"We have met in our dreams, Gordon. Don't you remember now?"

"I almost remember. But your name is just around the corner and away from me."

"I've never had a name . . . for you," she said. And then her face clouded. "But if I should tell you my name, it would spoil everything. You aren't going to ask me for that, dear?"

"How can a name spoil anything?"

"If I showed you my father's house, you would understand."

"If I should lose you, how could I trail you and find you again, if I did not know your name?"

"You could find the river, and the river will always bring you to me, you know. But we never can leave one another now. If we turn together and ride fast, they'll never overtake us . . . if we once get to the hills and ride down the valley road beside the river, just the way you came."

"I have never run away from any man or men," he answered sternly. "How can I run away now? Who will follow?"

"My father and all his men. Have you forgotten that?"

Fear grew up in Macdonald, but at the same time there was a wild desire to ride on to the end of that road. And as for "father and all his men," he was consumed with a perverse eagerness to see them. It was from this, then, that the river had bidden him turn back. But on he went, with the girl riding close beside him, beseeching him to stop.

When they came to the great avenue of walnut trees, they entered a village and passed through it until they came into a deep garden and straight under the façade of a lofty house, one of the largest he had ever seen, he thought, with great wooden turrets and gables. To Macdonald it looked like a castle.

"Is this your father's house, where he lives with all his men?" he asked of the girl.

But no voice answered him and, when he turned, the girl was gone. He looked on all sides, but she was nowhere to be seen.

They have stolen her away from me, he thought to himself. *They have taken her into the house and, if I follow her there, they will kill me, but if I do not follow her, I shall never see her again.* And it seemed to Macdonald that, if he never saw her again, it would be worse, far worse than death. For the sound of her voice he would have crossed a sea. And there was a soft slenderness to her hand, like the hand of a child, that took hold on his heart.

"If I follow her into the house," Macdonald said softly to himself, "I am no better than a dead man, but if I do not follow her, I am worse than dead."

So he marched resolutely up the winding path. He strode up the wide steps, but when he came before the door of the house, though he had not heard a sound of a footfall following him, a strong hand clutched him by the shoulder.

Swiftly he turned around, but there was nothing behind him save the empty air, and the grip of the hand held him by the shoulder, ground into the strength of his big muscles, and seemed biting him to the bone like a hand of fire.

Here Macdonald awoke. There was a hand

indeed upon his shoulder, and over his bed a dim figure was leaning. Instantly he grappled with the other, found his throat, dashed him to the floor.

"For Lord's sake," groaned the voice of the other, "don't kill me . . . it's only Jenkins."

V

So real had been the dream, so vivid had been the sunshine that he had seen in it, so clear the flowers and the trees and the shrubs in that great garden and the looming house above him, that for a moment the black darkness in the room seemed to stifle the big man.

Macdonald recalled himself and raised the groveling form of Jenkins to his feet.

"A fool thing to wake a man like that . . . in the middle of the night," he growled at Jenkins. "Wait till I light a lamp."

"Not a lamp, in the name of reason," panted the gambler. "Somebody might be watching . . . somebody might guess. . . ."

"Guess what?"

"That you put me up to the work."

"What work?"

"Playing with Rory Moore and breaking him."

The whole story rolled back upon the mind of Macdonald, and for a moment the face of the girl in his dream was dim. "Ah, yes," he said. "And tell me what happened?"

"You seen just what would happen, Macdonald. Moore played like a crazy man. I won so fast it had me dizzy. Finally he was broke. He put up his watch . . . he put up everything he had."

"Even the ranch?"

"Nope, it seems that he made that over to his sister. It's in her name."

"But he lost everything else?"

"Everything! And finally he put up Sunset. You'd have thought that he was staking his soul on them cards. And when he lost, he put his head between his hands and groaned like a sick kid."

"But you got the horse, Jenkins?"

"It's in the stable behind the hotel. I'm leaving the first thing in the morning. I'm going to tell them at the stable that I sold the horse to you. Then I light out for Canada."

"Why that?"

"Rory Moore may find out what I am, that some folks think I don't always play square with the cards. And if he thinks that he's been cheated out of that horse, he'll kill me, Macdonald! Why, he'd follow me around the world to sink a bullet into me."

"Shut up! You're talking like a woman, not a man. Be quiet, Jenkins. Go wherever you please, but let me have the horse. Good bye."

"Will you shake hands and wish me luck, Macdonald?"

"You card-juggling rat! I've used you, and I'm done with you. You have the money, and I have the horse. Now get out and never come back!"

He could feel Jenkins shrinking away from him through the darkness, and from the door he heard the stealthy whisper of the gambler.

"I dunno that I'm any worse than you. You put me up to this game. I dunno that I'm any worse than you."

"Bah!" sneered the big man. "Get out!" Then the door shut quickly behind the other.

After he had gone, the strangeness of the dream returned upon Macdonald. He lighted a lamp and sat down with his face between his hands, but he found that his heart was still beating wildly, and the face and the form of the girl still stayed in his thoughts more vividly, so it seemed, than when he had first seen her in the vision. There was none of the usual mistiness of dreams about her. He could remember the very texture of the sleeve of her riding habit. He could remember the way a wisp of hair, blown loose from beneath her stiff black hat, fluttered and swayed across her cheek. He could remember how her bay mare had danced and sidled, coming back down the avenue of the walnut trees. And, above all, he still held the quality of her voice in his ear. How she had pleaded with him not to approach that house behind the garden. And how mysteriously she had disappeared, when at last he had called to her. What might have happened had he not persisted in going on? And, above all, what was it that made him persist? What was the pull and the lure that drove him so irresistibly ahead?

At this he started up out of his chair with a stifled exclamation of disgust with himself. Of course anything was possible in a dream. There was no real existence except in his thoughts alone.

He stared around the room. It seemed to Macdonald that, if he could rest his eyes on some familiar daylight object, his nerves would quiet. But what his glance first encountered was the dark and faded portrait of an old gentleman with a white muffler—turned gray with age—around his throat, and one hand thrust pompously into the bosom of his coat. He smiled, and the smile was a grotesque caricature done in cracked paint. And the blue of his eyes was dim with time.

Daylight reality? There was more in one second of the dream than in an age of such pictures. And the whole room exuded a musty aroma of the past. Yonder dust, which lay in the corner, seemed to have lain there for a generation, and the footprint within it had been made by the foot of one long dead.

In vain Macdonald strove to rally from this obsession. In vain he told himself that this was no more than an old family mansion long used as a hotel—every room occupied many times in the course of each year. But the more he used his reason, the more it failed him.

The panic was growing momently in him, and it was a strange sensation. Not on that day, when the five men had cornered him in an Australian desert and held him, more dead than living, in a group of rocks for forty-eight hours, without water—not even in the worst of those hours had he felt this clammy thing called fear. There was a weakness in his stomach and in his throat. He felt that if a knock were to come at his door, there would hardly be in his knees sufficient strength to answer it. Suppose that in this condition some enemy were to find him and reach for a gun?

He shuddered strongly at that thought. Then, driven by a peculiar curiosity, he forced himself to go to the mirror and to hold above his head with shaking hands the lamp. What he saw was like the face of another man. The pupils of his eyes were dilated. His lips were drawn. His bronzed cheeks had turned a sickly yellow, and his forehead was glistening with perspiration. He put down the lamp with a muffled oath, then glanced sharply over his shoulder to the window, for it seemed to him as though his eyes, a moment before, had been watching him from its black rectangle, with the high light from the lamp thrown across it, blurring the outer dark.

After this he consulted his watch. It was half past two, and at this hour he certainly could not start his day's journey. But the very thought of remaining in that room was unspeakably horrible to him.

He dressed at once. There was Sunset, at least, waiting for him in the stable. At that thought half of the nightmare fears left him. He hurried through the packing of his bedroll, then left the room and went down the stairs. On the desk in the deserted little lobby he left more than enough to pay his bill. Then he started out for the stable.

It was deserted like the lower floor of the big house. Even the stable, which the Moores had built behind their home, was lofty and mansion-like, finished at the top with sky-reaching gables and adorned at the upper rim of the roof with an elaborate cornice of carved wood, half of whose figures had cracked away with the passage of the years and the lack of paint.

As he stepped through the great arch of the central door, he found a single lamp burning behind a chimney black with smoke. This he took as a lantern and examined the horses in the stalls. There were only five kept there for the night. The rest were in the corrals behind the building, and in the first of these corrals he found Sunset.

The stallion had been placed by himself and, the moment the lamp from the light struck on him, he came straight for the bearer, his big eyes as bright as two burning disks, and the lamplight was quivering and running along the silk of his red flanks.

Macdonald uttered a faint exclamation of delight. It was the first time in his wild life that he had secured anything through fraud. Treachery had never been one of his mental qualities. But, as the horse nosed at his shoulder and whinnied softly, as though they had been friends for many a year, his heart leaped. Every man, he had always felt, will commit one crime before his life was over, and this must be the crime of Macdonald. How much bloodshed, how many deaths could be laid to his score did not matter. He had risked his own life in taking the life of another. But here he had gone behind another man and cheated him with hired trickery.

It was very base. The whole soul of Macdonald revolted at the thought of Jenkins and the part he had played. But he would use Sunset as tenderly as any master could use him. That, at least, was certain.

In five minutes his saddle was on the back of the stallion, his roll was strapped to it, and he had vaulted into the stirrups and jogged out onto the main street of the town. There were no noises. The town slept the sleep of the mountains, black and stirless. The great stars were bright above him. And under him the stallion was dancing with eagerness to be off at full speed, dancing and playing lightly against the bit, but as smooth of action as running water.

He spoke gently, and Sunset was off into a breath-taking gallop, no pitch and pound, as of the range mustang, but a long and sweeping stride, as though the beat of invisible wings bore him up and floated him over the ground. They flashed out of town. Now the blackness of the plain lay before them, and Sunset was settling to his work. A horse? No, it was like sitting on the back of an eagle. The cold of the nightmare left him, and it seemed to Macdonald that, if he turned, he would see the girl of his vision cantering beside him, laughing up to him.

Now he touched Sunset with the spurs. It was half a mile before he could pull the startled horse out of a mad run and bring him into a canter again, with hand and voice soothing the stallion. By that time all thoughts of the dream were behind him. But for how long? When would she come again to make his heart ache with loneliness and to fill him again with the sad certainty of disaster toward which he was traveling?

One thing at least was necessary. He must find action—action that would employ him to the full. He must have battle such as he had never had before. He must fight against odds. He must plunge into danger as into cleansing waters, and these would wash the memory from his mind.

So at least it seemed to Macdonald, as he gnawed his lip and rode on into the night. And he cast around in his thoughts for an objective. It was no longer easy to find the danger which was the breath of his nostrils. Time had been when the shrug of a shoulder or a careless word would plunge him into battle. But that time had passed. His reputation had spread wide before him and men took far more from him than they would take from their ordinary fellows. Moreover, how many sheriffs had warned him solemnly that the next time there was a killing by him in their county, self-defense would be no defense, but he would be left to the mercy of the crowd?

He must find some ready-made trouble, and with that the inspiration came to him. Five years before in the town of Sudeth he had killed young Bill Gregory, and the Gregorys one and all had sworn that he would never live to spend another day in that town. What could be more perfect? He had only to ride into the town of Sudeth and take a room in the hotel. The next move would be up to the Gregorys. There were scores of them about the place, and they were not the type of men to forget past oaths.

VI

The tidings of his coming went out on wings, and that night the Gregorys assembled. In the course of two generations a large family had multiplied greatly and become almost a clan, of which the head was old Charles Gregory, and it was at his ranch house, a scant mile from the town of Sudeth, that the assembly gathered. Old or young, gray or dark, they packed into the big dining room. The elders sat. The younger men, the fighting van of the Gregory family, were ranged around the wall, smoking cigarettes until their faces were lost behind a haze, but speaking rarely or never. For it was felt in the Gregory family that age had its rights and its wisdom, and that young men may listen to them with profit.

Old Charles Gregory himself sat at the head of the board. Time had withered, but not faded, him. His arms and hands were shrunk like the arms and hands of a mummy, but his thin, bronzed cheek still held a healthful glow, and his eyes were as bright as the eyes of a youth. He opened the meeting with a little speech.

"There ain't no use saying why we've come together, folks," he said. "The hound has come back. It wasn't enough that we didn't follow him out and finish him off after he murdered poor Bill. That wasn't enough. We kept the law and stayed quiet. But being quiet only made him figure that he could walk right over us. So he's back here, sitting easy at the hotel and waiting for us to do something. The question is . . . what are we going to do?"

The elders around the table neither stirred nor spoke, but there was a slight and uneasy shifting of feet around the wall and a dull jingling of spurs. Not a man there was a man of action.

"None of you seem to have no ideas," Charles Gregory said fiercely. "But first off I'd better tell you just what happened when Bill was killed. There's been a lot of talk about it since. There's been five years for talk to grow up, and talk grows faster than any weed on the range. I'll tell you the facts because, come my time of life, the longer ago a thing happens the clearer it is to me."

He paused and closed his eyes. For the moment he looked like a weary mask of death. Now again his eyes looked out from the steep shadow of his brows, and he went on: "And you younger people listen close. You're going to hear the facts. It started over nothing, the way most shooting scrapes start. Bill comes riding into town one day and goes up on the verandah and sits down in a chair. Pretty soon Abe Sawyer comes up to him and says to him . . . 'You know who that chair belongs to?'

" 'I dunno,' says Bill.

" 'Gordon Macdonald has been sitting in it,' says Abe.

" 'Who's Gordon Macdonald?' says Bill.

" 'A nacheral born man-killer,' says Abe, 'and the worst man with a gun that ever was born.'

"Bill sits and thinks a minute.

" 'I don't know how much gunfighter he is,' says Bill, 'but he sure ain't got this chair mortgaged. If he happens to sit down in it in the morning, he ain't going to have it kept for him here all day.'

"Abe didn't say no more about it. He went off and sat down to watch, and pretty soon a big man comes out through the door of the hotel and taps Bill on the shoulder.

" 'Excuse me, partner,' he says, 'but this is my chair.'

"Bill answers without turning his head. 'Do you think that you can hold down a chair all day by just sitting in it once?'

" 'I was fixing my spurs,' says the big man, 'and I left one of 'em lying on each side of the chair. Ain't that enough to hold down a chair for a man for two minutes? Besides, there's other chairs out here on the porch, and you could have sat in one of them, couldn't you?'

"Bill looks down and he sees the spurs for the first time. He looks up to the face of Macdonald, and he said later that it was like looking up into the face of a lion. His nerve sort of faded out of him.

" 'Maybe you're right,' he says, and gets up and takes another chair. But, while he's sitting in the other chair, he sees half a dozen of the gents that have watched the whole thing sort of looking at him and then at one another and smiling. A shiver runs up Bill's spine, and he starts asking himself if they think he's taken water. He's got half a mind to go over and pick a fight with Macdonald right there, to show that he has nerve enough to suit any man. But then he remembers that he's going to marry poor Jenny inside of a week, and he decides that he ain't got no right to fight a gunman.

"He goes on home. As soon as he sits down to the supper table, in comes his cousin, Jack, over yonder . . . oh, Jack, it was a poor part you played that night . . . and started joking with Bill because he'd give up his chair to Macdonald. Bill didn't say a word to nobody. But he gets up from the table and goes out and saddles a horse and starts for Sudeth town. He runs down the street, jumps off'n his horse, and dives into the hotel. There he looks up this Macdonald. He starts in cussing Macdonald, with his hand on the butt of his gun. He says that Macdonald must have started talking about him and calling him yellow. But Macdonald talks back to him plumb soft and says that he don't want no trouble, and that the matter about the chair don't mean nothing. Pretty soon Bill got to thinking that *Macdonald* was yellow, I guess, from the soft way that Macdonald talks. Anyways he goes up and punches Macdonald on the jaw. Macdonald knocks him down. While Bill lies on the floor, he pulls his gun, and Macdonald waits till he sees the steel, then he pulls his own Colt like a flash and kills poor Bill."

Charles Gregory paused, looking down to his withered hands, clasped above the table. There was no sound in the room.

"That's the straight of that killing of Bill, and it sounds like Bill was simply a fool. But since then we've heard a lot about Macdonald, and we know that he's one of these gents that goes around hunting trouble, and when he gets into trouble, he backs up and talks soft and tries to make the other gent lead at him, but the minute anything is started, Macdonald does all the finishing. He lives on murder. We've traced him a ways, and we've planted twenty dead men to his credit. Now, folks, this Macdonald is the man we told to get out of Sudeth and never come back, and here he is in town again. I seen the sheriff today. All he said was that he had a long trip to make and was leaving *pronto*, which was the same as saying that he knew that Macdonald was a plumb bad one, and that he wouldn't dislike having us wipe him out. Ain't I right? The only question is . . . how are we going to do it?"

There was a small, respectful pause at the conclusion of this speech, and finally Henry Gregory, a wide-shouldered, gray-headed man, spoke from the farther end of the table. No one in that room was more respected by the others.

"I've had my storms," he said, "and I've done my fighting. But the older I get the more I figure that no good can come out of the muzzle of a Colt with a Forty-Five slug. And I say short and *pronto* . . . no more fighting. Let Macdonald stay. Poor Bill is dead. There ain't no doubt that it was no better than murder. There ain't no doubt that this Macdonald is a professional, and before we could get rid of him, a couple of our boys are sure to go down. I say . . . hands off of Macdonald."

"There'd be a lot of talk!" exclaimed half a dozen voices in a chorus.

"Nobody but a fool would accuse the Gregorys of being cowards," said Henry. "What fools say don't bother us none. We can let 'em chatter."

Someone stepped forward from the wall of the room with a clank of spurs. It was the face of Jack Gregory that came out of the mist of smoke.

"Folks," he said, "I'd ought to wait until my elders have finished talking, maybe, but I got something to say that needs saying pretty bad. Grandfather Charles was sure right when he said that it was me joking Bill that sent him into town to fight. God knows that I didn't mean no harm. Me and Bill was always pals, everybody knows.

But it was me that got Bill killed, and I'll never live it down with myself. What I got to say is this. Let me go in and face the music. Let me meet Macdonald and try my luck. It's my business."

There was a stern hum of dissent, and Mack Gregory, the father of Jack, turned and glanced gloomily at his son.

"No," said old Charles Gregory, speaking again, "we've passed our word that Macdonald should never come back to Sudeth, and he's done it. Right or wrong, we've passed our word. It ain't the business of Jack. It's the business of all of us. Speaking personal, I say that it would be suicide to send only one man. We need more. Macdonald is a lion."

There was another growl of agreement.

"Are we going to let folks say that the Gregorys have to fight in twos?" protested Henry Gregory, but he was not heard.

In another moment they were busy preparing the lots and then making the draw. By weird chance it fell upon both the sons of the peace-maker, Henry Gregory. Steve and Joe were his only children, great-boned, silent fellows, as swarthy of skin as Indians and as terrible as twin wildcats in a fight. Certainly the choice could not have fallen upon two more formidable men.

"But it ain't right," protested Jack. "I sure ought to have a hand. If Steve and Joe are hurt, the blame of it will come back on me, and I can't stand it."

"Shut up!" snarled his father. "You're playing the fool, Son. Are you wiser than all the rest of us?"

So Jack was cried down, but his mind was not put at rest by all the talk. He heard it decided that the attack on Macdonald should be made in the morning. He heard the farewells as the party broke up. And, witnessing all these things through a mist, all he saw clearly was the stern face of Henry Gregory, now wan with sorrow for his sons. He saw that, and it determined him on the spot. He waited until the assembly had scattered, then he took his horse, fell to the rear, and presently had turned down a path and started for the town of Sudeth.

VII

In the meantime, Macdonald had waited until the night. Yet it was not wasted time. In anticipation he was turning over the danger in his mind, as a connoisseur turns over the thought of the expected feast. He had put his head into the jaws of the lion, as he was well aware. How those jaws would close was the fascinating puzzle. They might attack him by surprise, or in a crowd. They might wait for the night, and then they would be truly terrible, or else they might strike boldly in the day, when he would have a better fighting chance.

Such surmises filled his mind all the late morning. In the early afternoon he fell asleep and, the instant he closed his eyes, he was once more traveling up the river in the mountains, with the voice forming out of the sounding current—"Turn back! Turn back! Turn back!" in endless reiteration. Once more he climbed to the headwaters of the stream. He crossed the divide. And he saw before him the same sunny plain, exactly as it had been before.

He wakened suddenly, and that afternoon he slept no more, but went down into the lobby of the hotel and then onto the verandah in front, where there would be other men around him.

The evening came, and still there was no sign of the coming of the Gregorys. But word was brought to him that the sheriff had left the town. And then new word came that the Gregorys were meeting that evening. For, wherever Macdonald went, though he had no friends and no companions, there was always a certain number of men, like the jackals who follow the king of beasts, ready to carry information to the great man, ready to cringe and cower before his greatness. He treated them, as they needed to be treated, with a boundless contempt, but on occasion they were invaluable to him. They were very necessary on this day, for instance, with their eager whispers to and fro. And it was one of these fellows who brought the word about Rory Moore.

"If anybody was to ask me where there was going to be trouble first," said this sneak of an informant, "I'd say it would come right here in Sudeth. And the second place it's going to come is to Rory Moore in his own town."

"Rory Moore? Rory Moore?" Macdonald said sharply. "What the devil do you know about him?"

"Nothing but what everybody will know pretty *pronto*. I ain't doing you no favor telling you this. Twenty men could tell it to you pretty soon. Rory Moore is telling folks around his home town that you stole his horse, Sunset, from him."

It brought a growl from Macdonald, and he dropped his cigarette to the floor and smashed it with his heel.

"I stole his horse? It's a lie! I bought it from a man who won Sunset from him in a gambling game."

"It was a frame-up," said the informer. "Moore swears it was a frame-up. He says that he's found out that Jenkins, who won the horse from him, was really a professional gambler, a crooked player whose real name is Vincent. Is that right, Macdonald?"

"Hang Jenkins and Moore both!" cried

Macdonald. "Where does all this rot come from?"

"The telephones have been packed with it all morning. Seems that this fellow Vincent . . . was it really Vincent?"

"What if it was?"

"Nothing except that Vincent is an old hand. He was run out of Sudeth a couple of years back, and he's been tarred and feathered a couple of times for his dirty work with the cards. And one of these days they'll talk to him with a gun, they will. Anyway, it seems that this Jenkins, as he was calling himself, started right out of town after he'd cleaned Rory Moore up at the cards. But early the next morning Moore heard some talk about town that Jenkins was really Vincent, the crooked gambler. It took Moore about one second to see through everything, the way he'd lost the night before. He started on Jenkins's trail. By noon he'd run him down. He put a gun on Jenkins, and the hound got down and crawled and said he'd confess everything, if Moore would let him live.

"So Moore let him live, and Jenkins told him a crazy yarn. Said that you'd come to Jenkins the night before and found him broke. You offered to stake him to five hundred dollars, if he'd use it to clean out Moore and make him put up his horse at the end of the game. The horse was what you wanted. You'd tried to buy it, and when Moore wouldn't sell, you schemed to get Sunset

270

this way. And the scheme worked, according to Jenkins. He got the money and the horse. He put the horse in the stable, told you where it was, and then run for his life. And Moore swears that you rode out of town before morning, which shows that you were afraid to stay. Anyway, he got all his money back from Jenkins, and now he's hunting across country to find you and Sunset. I'm wondering if he'll have a hard time finding you?"

Here the speaker laughed hugely at the poor jest, but Macdonald found the story no laughing matter. If this story were out, if this story were proved—and who could doubt the confession of Jenkins, alias Vincent, the card shark?—then Macdonald would be established in the eyes of the men of the ranges not only as a man-slayer, but as a scheming rascal, and men who would never combine against one who merely took lives could immediately gather together to run to earth a crafty schemer. Decidedly it was tidings of the most serious import. Macdonald gritted his teeth, as he thought it over. If he could tear Vincent to small pieces and scatter the remnants to the dogs, there would be some satisfaction. But Vincent was a poor mongrel not worthy of a blow.

Meantime, there was a pleasanter side to the story. Of all the men he had faced in the past half dozen years, there had been none to compare with Rory Moore in dash and spirit. He had not the slightest doubt that the young rancher was a warrior of parts. And a battle against him would be a pleasure distinctly worth a search of a thousand miles. If he came alive from this affair at Sudeth, he would be instantly back in Moore's hometown and await him there in the hotel. What could be better than that? And in wiping out Moore, he would wipe out the person chiefly interested in telling that ugly tale about the crooked gambler's work.

It was evening, and he was back in the lobby before he came to all of those conclusions. And they were hardly formed, when his attention was sharply called by a silence that had fallen over the room. There was a soft and sudden shifting of positions. Macdonald, looking into a small mirror that was hanging on the wall in front of him—a little diamond-shaped affair meant to be a decoration—saw a big fellow striding through the door and into the room. He did not need more than one glance to make sure that this was a man come on desperate business. The pale, rather drawn face, the glaring eyes, the jaw set hard and thrust out a little, were all the features of a man on the verge of meeting death itself.

"Macdonald!" called the stranger.

As Macdonald rose slowly from his chair, he stretched his arms.

"Look out!" gasped the voice of the human jackal who had brought him so much news that day. "Look out! It's Jack Gregory, and he's a fighting fool!"

But Macdonald turned with glorious unconcern. "Calling me?" he asked cheerfully.

"I'm calling you. Macdonald, I want to talk to you outside the hotel."

Macdonald hesitated. One who dreaded Macdonald's speed and his accuracy with a gun often sought to equalize matters a little more by bringing him into the darkness. But, after all, he had fought a score of times in the light of the stars. He had made a point of doing as much target practice by night as by day, and the chances, which were heavy against any foe in the daylight, were even heavier against them in the dark. After that moment of delay he nodded and crossed the room to the other.

"I don't think I remember meeting you," he said.

"You don't," said the other. "My name is Jack Gregory."

And, as he spoke, his body drew stiff and straight and his right hand trembled near to the butt of his gun. But such a killing was by no means in the mind of Macdonald. With the blandest of smiles he held out his hand.

"Very glad to meet you, Gregory," he said.

His hand was disregarded.

"I want to talk with you outside. Will you come?"

"Certainly."

They passed through the door and descended the steps. They stood in the street. Instantly the door of the hotel was packed with a blur of white faces, watching eagerly. Macdonald looked about him with infinite satisfaction. It was a moonless night, to be sure. The moon would not be up for another hour, but the sky was clear, and the stars were shining as clear as crystal. Certainly there was light enough for Macdonald to shoot almost as straight as by daylight, at such close range. But what was this Gregory saying?

"Macdonald," he said, "I've come to beg you to leave town."

"Beg me to leave it?" Macdonald asked with the slightest and most insulting emphasis.

"Just that," said the other.

"And if I don't go?"

"We fight."

"I'm sorry to hear that," said Macdonald, and in the starshine he smiled evilly upon Jack Gregory. "But as for leaving," he continued, "you must admit that this is a free country and a free town. Why should I leave, if you please?"

"Because," Gregory explained, "my family has sworn that you cannot stay here."

"Interesting," said the mild, soft voice of the man-killer, "but unimportant, Gregory."

"Macdonald," pleaded the other, "it was some fool joking of mine that drove Bill Gregory, five years ago, to come in and have it out with you. I got his death on my conscience. Now some of the rest of the boys are going to try to get you out of town, but it ain't their business. It's mine. If you should kill them, their ghosts would haunt me. So I've come in to try to persuade you."

"I'm listening," said Macdonald.

"Everybody on the range knows that you're a brave man, Macdonald. If you leave town, nobody'll think any the worse of you, and I'll let the folks know that I asked you to go and didn't drive you out by threats."

"Who'd believe you?" asked Macdonald grimly, as he saw the bent of the conversation. "You'd get a big reputation cheap. But what would I get?"

"A cold thousand. I've saved that much, and . . ."

"You fool!"

"Listen to me, Macdonald. I'm not trying to insult you, but I'm trying to think of everything in the world to persuade you. If you don't want the money, forget that I mentioned it. But I'm desperate. I know that I can't stand up to you, but if you won't go by persuasion, I got to try my gun."

It was a situation unique in the experience of Macdonald, and he hesitated. But what cause had he to love the world or trust or pity any man in it? From the very first his life had been a battle.

"If I gave way," he explained coldly, "I'd have

twenty men ready to bully me wherever I went. The story would go around that you'd bluffed me, Gregory. I'd rather be dead than be shamed."

There was a groan from Gregory. "You cold-hearted devil!" he cried. "If there's no other way, I'll try my luck!"

Gregory reached for his gun. Even then there was time for Macdonald to seem to protest—for the benefit of those who were jammed in the doorway of the hotel. He raised a hand in that protest, and he called loud enough for the spectators to hear: "Not that, Gregory!"

Macdonald saw the gun of the other flash. It was shooting at ten paces, and even a poor shot was not apt to miss him. He dropped his right hand on the butt of his gun, making it swing up, holster and all, for the end of the holster was not steadied against his thigh. At the same instant he pulled the trigger. Jack Gregory spun and dropped. He had been shot squarely between the eyes.

VIII

No doubt, when all was said and done, it was as fair a fight as had ever been seen in the town of Sudeth. There was no shadow of a doubt that Jack Gregory had pressed home the battle. There was no doubt that he had reached first for his gun, and that the odium of beginning the fight rested entirely on him. But, in spite of this, there was a roar of anger from the spectators when they saw him fall.

They were out through the doorway in a rush, and every man had a drawn gun in his hand. A moment before they had been watching as spectators at a game. Suddenly they realized that in this game the prize was death, and that Jack Gregory had received it—Jack Gregory who every man there, perhaps, had known from his boyhood. His life was wasted, and yonder was the man of fame, the cool slayer, who had conquered again. And the horror of it took them suddenly by the throat.

One section of that little mob spilled out toward the body of Gregory, lying face down in the dust. The other section swarmed toward the slayer.

"Finish the murdering dog!" someone was crying.

"Hold him for the sheriff!" called another.

"And see him get free on self-defense?" was the answer. "No, we'll be our own law! Macdonald, put up your hands!"

There had been no chance to run. In that clear starlight with a dozen guns covering him, Macdonald knew that he could not get away. Therefore he stood his ground, and at the order he obediently thrust his arms above his head, not straining them high up, as men in fear will do, but holding them only a trifle above the height of his shoulders, standing at ease and facing the rush of the mob.

"He's dead!" cried voices from the rear. "Poor old Jack is dead. He'll never speak again. That murdering hound has sure got to pay for this!"

They joined the circle around Macdonald.

"Get iron on his wrists."

"No irons here. A rope will do. Where's a rope?"

"Here's one!"

"Your sheriff will hunt you down," said Macdonald.

"Do you think that a jury could be found in this country that would convict a man for helping to lynch you?" someone asked, and Macdonald felt the truth of the query.

"Put down your hands, one hand at a time," commanded the man with the rope. "Jab a gun into his middle, a couple of you, and kill him if he tries to move."

Macdonald smiled down upon them. Perhaps this was a little more than he had bargained for, but it was not at all unpleasant. The old tingling joy in peril, which he had found so early in his life and loved so long, was thrilling in him now. They had his life upon the triggers of a dozen guns and yet, if he could strike suddenly enough, their very numbers . . .

He did not pause to complete that thought. He

had been lowering his right hand slowly toward the rope, as though to show that he intended no sudden effort to escape. Now he jerked it down and knocked away two revolvers that had been thrust against his body. One of them exploded, and there was a yell of pain from a bystander when the bullet plowed through his leg. At the same instant half a dozen pairs of arms reached for Macdonald, but he spun around. Their fingers slipped on the hard bulk of his muscles. And now he drove ahead, crouching low, as a football player charges a line. They tumbled away before him like snow before a snowplow. Who could fire, when the bullet, nine chances out of ten, would find lodgment in the body of a friend?

They poured after Macdonald, but two or three had lost their footing and gone down. They entangled some of those who followed. Now there was a sudden thinning of the mass before Macdonald. Two men stood before him. He smote one on the side of his head, saw the head rebound, as though broken at the neck, and the man went down. His shoulder, as he rushed, crashed against the breast of the other, and the man fell with a gasp. There was an open way before Macdonald, and he went down it, like a racing deer with the sound of the hounds behind it.

With a sweep they followed, but before they had taken half a dozen steps, they saw he was stepping swiftly away from them, and the leaders stopped to shoot. But a fight, a scramble, a race, and the starlight, combined with the knowledge that one is shooting at a famous target, make a very poor effect upon the nerves. The shower of bullets flew wild. Macdonald ran on unscathed. He reached the corner of the hotel and whipped around it. He headed down the side of the building, then darted for the corrals, with the mob still in hot pursuit. But they lost at every fence, for he leaped them in stride, like the athlete that he was, and they had to pause to crawl between the rails or vault over.

He found Sunset at once. Onto his back he vaulted, and it seemed that the fine animal knew at once what was expected of him. A tap on the side of the neck turned him around, and a word started him away at a flying gallop. He took the fence with a wild leap that brought a yell of despair and rage from the pursuers and in another moment he was sunk in the outer blackness of the night.

They pursued him no more than one would attempt to overtake an arrow after seeing it leave the string. But Macdonald had not left to stay away that night. He galloped not half a mile, then returned and headed straight back to the hotel. Into it he ventured, stole up the back stairs, and got to his room. They had not touched his belongings. He packed them deliberately, returned down the stairs, went out to the shed and got his saddle and bridle, put them on Sunset, and was again ready for the journey.

As for the town of Sudeth, it passed through a sudden and violent transition. For two hours they raved against the cool-handed murderer and swore that they would run him to the earth, if it took them a life of labor to do the task. But at the end of the two hours, a committee went up to investigate the belongings of Macdonald and found them gone. On the plaster of the wall was written:

A very pleasant party.
Macdonald

When the others learned, there was a storm of wonder and then of appreciation. For they had heard enough to convince them that there was something almost supernal in the courage of a man who could return on the heels of the very mob that was hunting his life. There and then the townsmen lost their interest in the chase of Macdonald. That was left to the Gregorys, and the Gregorys solemnly took up the trail.

IX

No seer was needed to tell Macdonald that the town of Sudeth was apt to lose its enthusiasm for war before long, but that the clan of Gregorys would never leave him until they had clashed at least a few more times. Nevertheless he had no desire to put a great distance between himself and his probable pursuers. There was first the little matter with Rory Moore that was to be settled. And he let Sunset run like a homing bird straight across the hills toward home.

They reached it nearly a day later, in the red time of sunset, with all the town as hushed and peaceful as a pictured place rather than a reality. He saw one old man smoking a pipe at the door of a shop. He heard in the weird distance one dog barking. But of living sights and sounds, these were the only two. The town might have died. It was like riding into the ghost of a place.

Of course it was easily explainable, Macdonald told himself. The people were simply at supper and, since they all kept the same hour for supper, they would all be off the streets at that time. And yet such a conclusion did not entirely satisfy him. There was a solemnity about this quiet, this utter silence, with the far-off wailing of the dog, that warned him back like the voice of the river in his dream.

At the hotel he found the same sleepy atmosphere that he had noted before in the place. The hotel, in short, was not paying. For in spite of its size and the comfort of its arrangement, there was a forbidding atmosphere about the place that had held the trade away. Macdonald felt it again as he stood in front of the desk in the hotel office and asked for a room. He would have given a good deal if he had not come to this hostelry where he had spent that terrible night so short a time before. He would have given a great deal if he had chosen, instead, the little shack that had been built at the farther end of the street, and which also went by the name of a hotel in the town.

But he could not withdraw, having come so far. He could not mumble and excuse and retreat. But his absent-mindedness, which was the curse of his life, having brought him on thus far, he must go on with the thing. He heard a cheerful promise that he should not only have a room, but that he should also have that very same room that he had occupied the last time he stayed there, the room that he had left so suddenly in the middle of the night.

And even from this proposal he could not dissent. He was kept quiet by the very violence of his feelings. How could he declare that the very last place on earth in which he wished to spend another night was the room where he had slept before? They might pin him down to the truth. They might discover—oh, monstrous joke to be roared at by the whole world—that Macdonald had run away from a dream like any brain-sick youth of fourteen years.

So he had to submit and was led upstairs to the room. When the door closed upon him, and he was left among its shadows, the old panic swept upon him. He could not stay there alone. Down the stairs he went again and out to the stable to look at Sunset. The stallion was digesting a liberal feed of grain and sweet-smelling hay. Half a dozen hungry chickens, roaming abroad in search of forage, were clustered around the outskirts of the pile of hay, scratching a quay into it and picking busily at the heads of grain. But the big stallion, when he had finished his grain and turned to the hay, made not the slightest objection to these small intruders. For he kept on steadily at his hay, merely cocking one sharp ear when the beak of a hen picked a little too close to that soft muzzle of his.

Macdonald hung over the fence of the corral, delighted, until the gathering of the shadows drove even those hungry chickens away from the hay and back to their roosting places.

"Yep," said a voice to the side, "that's a plumb easy-going horse, I'd tell a man."

Macdonald looked askance with a scowl. It

was by no means his habit to be so rapt in any observation that he allowed other men to stalk up beside him and take him by surprise. What he found was a little old man, very bent, so that his head was thrust far in front of his body, and he balanced himself with a round-headed cane on which his brown hands rested. He carried a short-stemmed pipe between his gums and puffed noisily at it. In a word he was like a figure out of a book, or off the stage.

"And who might you be?" asked the little man, and he had a quick, bird-like way of jerking his head toward the one to whom he was speaking, while he sucked on his pipe.

"Oh, I've just happened by," Macdonald murmured smoothly enough.

"You've heard that he's back again, I reckon," said the other. "You've come like me to have a look at Sunset before that Macdonald man rides him away again. I disremember when I seen a finer horse than Sunset."

"Nor I!" exclaimed Macdonald, and at the sound of his deep voice the stallion looked up, swung halfway toward his new master, and then allowed the greed of a big appetite to draw him back toward his fodder. But the heart of Macdonald was beating with a great new tenderness.

"The horse likes you," piped the old man. "Well, I never seen a horse yet that would waste a look on a bad man. All that makes me sorry is to think about Sunset being wasted on a man-killing, law-spoiling hound like that Macdonald."

"Is he as bad as that?" Macdonald asked slowly.

"He's worse," said the other with great venom, and he even removed his pipe from his mouth so that he might speak with more vehemence. Macdonald saw that the stem was wound with string to give a better grip to the old gums of the man. "He's a pile worse. There ain't nobody can say anything bad enough about him. What would you say about a gent that kills just for the sake of killing?"

"Why," Macdonald responded, "I think that depends on how he kills. Every man is a hunter, if you come down to that. They're all trying to kill one another, you know. But some are lucky, and some aren't so lucky. It depends, I say, on how he kills. If he takes as big a chance as the next man, what's so terribly wrong in that?"

"Suppose he killed with poison?"

"Do you mean to say that he does that?" cried Macdonald.

"Just as bad as that. He's such a good shot, and his nerves are so plumb steady, that he knows he ain't running no real risk when he faces another man. There ain't one chance in a hundred that he'll get so much as scratched. That's why I say he might as well use poison for his killings. And to think that a horse like Sunset . . ."

But Macdonald heard no more. He had listened to too much already, as a matter of fact, and he climbed back to his room with a heavy heart. And on the way he fought over the truth about himself. It had not occurred to him to look at the matter from this new viewpoint. He had always felt that it was fair fighting. But now that he thought of it, how clearly he saw the new idea. His skill, he had to confess, was far greater than the skill of the average man. Just how much chance *did* the other fellow have, when matched against the practiced hand and the familiar gun of Macdonald?

He thought back to many of his conflicts. In the old days he had been often wounded. His body was still ripped and dotted with scars. Yes, he had been wounded almost as often as he had wounded others. Finally he had gone into a fight almost expecting to have his own body wounded, or the life shot out of him. But, as time went on, he learned new things, and among the rest he learned to practice with his weapons assiduously every day. How long had it been now, since an enemy had wounded him in a fair fight, face to face? And what did that mean?

It meant that the old man standing by the corral had been right. He might as well have killed by poison.

He threw himself down upon his bed and, staring up into the darkness, his mind filled with two thoughts—the girl of whom he had dreamed, and the men who had fallen before him in his life of fighting. And so fiercely did he concentrate that in another moment he was riding up a river among the mountains, a river whose voice gathered into human words: "Turn back! Turn back! Turn back!"

X

So sudden had been that sleep that even in his dream he was acutely conscious of something left behind him, of a change just made. One half of his mind was trying to turn back to what he had been, while the other half was listening to the shouting of the river. At length he gave all his attention to the road before him.

It was all as it had been before. He rode to the top of the divide, where the water dwindled to a little spring. He looked over the plain onto a great sweep of sunshine and shadow, with browsing cattle, and the faint sounds of their lowing was blown to him upon the height. And, as before, even while looking at that pleasant and warm scene, a chill of distress passed into the heart of Macdonald with a wild misgiving of something that was to come. For the voice which God or a demon had put into that river could not be wrong. This was the third time he had ridden up that river to its rising, and on this third time there was certain to be a revelation of the catastrophe.

Yet turn back he could not. A nameless eagerness filled him, far overbalancing his fear. And down the hill he swept and over the meadow at the long-reaching gallop of the red stallion. So he came in due time to the same avenue of the walnut trees, under which he had passed before. And down that avenue he rode, with the growing dread that he had felt when he galloped there before, and yet with a wild desire to hear the beat of approaching hoofs and to see once more the girl riding around the sweep of the trees.

He reached that turn, but she did not come. He went on more slowly. He came again to the town, all quiet under the sun. He came again to the garden. And he stood once more before the great castle of a house where, as he remembered, a hand had fallen upon his shoulders, and the girl had disappeared. Perhaps she would come to him again now.

Slowly he went up the steps, and the great house before him was wonderfully silent. There was a flutter of wings, as a bird darted under the roof of the porch, brushed close to his face, and darted out again. Then he knocked at the door. It was opened so quickly that it was obvious that his approach had been noted, and that there was someone ready to let him in.

Yet he saw no one inside the dark, high hall

of the place. He stepped in and, the moment he did so, he discovered who had opened the door for him. It was a man whose hand was still on the knob, and he was standing flat against the wall. And the pale face was the face of Anthony Legrange, as he had been on that night eight years before, when he died in Cheyenne with a bullet from the gun of Macdonald through his heart. He had not altered by a single shade, save that he had been a gloomy man in those days, and now he was smiling, a calm smile of mockery and scorn, as though he had a knowledge before which Macdonald was as helpless as a child.

Macdonald reached hastily for his gun, but the smile of Anthony Legrange merely deepened and suddenly Macdonald knew that a gun would be of no avail to him in this house.

"Anthony," he said, "I thought that you were dead eight long years ago. But I'm a thousand times glad to see that I was wrong. A thousand times glad, old man!"

But the smile of Anthony merely deepened again. He closed the door and leaned his shoulders against it, facing Macdonald once more, as though he defied him to try to break out.

"Why," Macdonald said, frowning, "if you think that you've trapped me here, it makes no difference to me. Do you imagine that I'm afraid of you, Anthony? No, nor of a thousand like you."

At once he turned his back on Anthony, stepped into the next room, and passed through this to a great dining hall. There he found a long table set, the longest table he had ever seen, and all around it men were seated, and before them food was placed. Some were eating, and some were drinking, and some were smoking, so that the air was blue with smoke. Yet, though Macdonald walked through a cloud of it, he smelled not the least taint of tobacco.

He noted, too, that though they seemed all to be laughing and talking, they were not making any sound, and the fall of knives and forks upon the plates made no sound. It was very strange, but stranger than anything they did were their faces. For there were men from a dozen nations, and everyone, he saw, was a man who he had killed.

Yes, just before him sat young Jack Gregory, and with no mark of the mortal wound upon his forehead. And at the side of Gregory sat a great Negro, a giant of his kind, naked to the waist, just as he had been on that night, so many years before, when he had grappled with Macdonald in the fire room of the tramp freighter. That had been a grim battle. And it rushed back clean and clear upon the mind of Macdonald. He saw the Negro, blood streaming down his face, tear himself away. He saw the big fellow snatch up a great bar of iron used for trimming the fires. He saw himself catch up a lump of coal and with a true aim knock down the big stoker. He saw them grapple again, and his big hands had found a firm grip upon the throat of the black man.

And beside the Negro sat a hideous Malay, with a split upper lip, rolling his wild eyes, as he talked. That was the human devil who had leaped upon him from behind in an alley in Bombay.

Yonder was the burly English mate who had striven to enforce obedience by the weight of his fists. They had grappled and gone over the rail together. Macdonald had come up, but the mate had sunk.

Sitting side by side, yellow of skin and dark of eyes, were the Arizona Kid and his two brothers. Macdonald had trailed them when he was a Ranger, and he had killed them all in one glorious and bloody battle. Now the Arizona Kid pointed him out, and his two brothers laughed in the face of their slayer. Indeed, the whole table was laughing and pointing, until the perspiration rolled down the face of Macdonald.

He stepped to the table and struck upon it. The dishes jumped beneath the vibration of the stroke, but there was no jingling sound.

"You rattle-headed fools!" cried Macdonald. "Why do you laugh and point? I've sent you to damnation, every one of you, and I'd send you there again and think nothing of it! What are you doing here? What right have you in this place?

I had no fear of you living. Do you think for an instant that I'll be afraid of you because you come back after death and gibber at me?"

The Negro giant leaned across toward him and extended a long, black arm, and along the naked skin the highlights glimmered. Macdonald could see the bull throat expand and quiver, he could see the chest of the monster rise, and he waited for the immense voice which, on a day, had been strong enough to stun the ears of men. But, instead, there ran forth only the faintest of faint whispers, hardly discernible.

"We're laughing at you, Macdonald, because we have gone to hell, every one of us, but a worse man than any one of us killed us. You saved us, Macdonald, with your gun, and that's why we laugh at you."

"You lie!" thundered Macdonald. "Half of you were good men, and hell had no claim on that many of you. There's Jack Gregory at your side. What wrong had he ever done?"

He saw Jack Gregory convulsed with soundless laughter. Then he half rose and pointed an exultant arm at Macdonald.

"I was damned black until you saved me," he cried, and this time the sound that reached Macdonald was as faint as the ghost of an echo. "I'd forsworn myself to a girl that I got with a false marriage, and then I left her to take care of herself and her child. But I was killed by a worse man than I am, Macdonald, and that's why I laugh."

Macdonald stood back from the table, sick at heart.

"What have I done, then?" he cried to them. "I've fought every man of you fairly, squarely, face to face. I took no advantage. I never struck a man that was down. I never shot a man that wasn't fighting back. I never harmed a man that asked for mercy. Why am I worse than you?"

But instead of answering, they fell into a hearty convulsion of that shadowy laughter, and Macdonald strode from the room. At the very threshold of the next apartment he was greeted by the delicate sweetness of flowers, and now he saw that they were banked everywhere about the room. There were flowers of every kind, little wild flowers and crimson roses and great smudges of violets. The air was alive with their fragrance. He could not decipher one scent from another, for all was a blended sweetness.

And with the fragrance went a profound silence. It was like that weighty quiet that lies in the high regions of the mountains, when no noise seemed strong enough to break it. For no matter how loud, the sound comes deadened upon the ear, and the thick silence rolls in swiftly behind it and drowns the echoes, as they come flocking from the distant peaks. Such was the quiet in that room, a bewildering and awful thing.

In the center of the apartment stood an open coffin on a flower-clad pedestal, and in that coffin lay the dead. The profile was clearly to be seen, and it was the face of Rory Moore—Rory Moore dead before he had been struck! Rory Moore dead, and above him leaned the lady of the vision, still in her riding costume. Her lips trembled, and though no sound came from them, the tears streamed steadily down her face.

But that was not all Macdonald saw in that room of sorrow, for he made out that the face of the girl and the face of Rory Moore were wonderfully alike. They could not be more similar, save that what was drawn on a large and manly scale in Rory's dead face, was made small and exquisitely beautiful in the living face of the girl.

"It was not I!" cried Macdonald. "I swear to heaven that I have not touched him!"

At his voice she looked up. There was one glimpse for him of the horror and hatred in her eyes, and then with her raised eyes she shut out the sight of him.

And Macdonald wakened and found himself on his knees in the darkness of his room, with his arms stretched out before him, and his voice moaning vague words.

XI

Instantly Macdonald hurried down to Sunset. He only paused to sweep his pack together before he was gone, and on the way he looked at the time. He noted with a shudder that it was half past two, the exact hour at which he had last left his chamber. Beyond a doubt a curse had fallen upon this house.

In the corral he roused the stallion with a word, and led him into the stable, and in the light of a lantern put on the saddle. While his swift fingers worked, he made up his mind. To leave the town would make it seem that he had lost his nerve at last, and that he dared not wait for the coming of Rory Moore. But let that be as it might. He must go nevertheless. For, if he met Rory Moore, nothing could keep him from killing the younger man, and kill Rory he must not. No, all the superstition in his strange soul urged him against it. He had received a warning, and that warning must be heeded.

Plunging into the darkness he headed away from the town, and he rode on until morning came. It was no sooner light than he camped by the way. By midmorning his sleep was ended, and Sunset was rested. He went on again. All that day he struck blindly ahead, and by nightfall he came into the heart of the mountains.

He had paid not the least heed to direction. He only knew that he was covering many miles, and that was sufficient. He went on from the second camp before the next day had well begun. By this time Rory Moore would have heard of his coming to the town, would have returned, found him gone, and would have published him abroad as a coward. But that was still a small thing in the mind of Macdonald. For the girl of his dreams was more to him now than all the rest of the living world. She had lived in his mind and in his very heart. She was never absent from him. And he found himself, a hundred times in the day, grown tense with waiting for her voice. And he found himself hurrying Sunset toward the rise of every hill in eagerness to see her coming.

It was just after he had camped to make coffee at noon and had gone on again that he found the place. He had come over a ridge, and journeying down to the sound of the waters he came suddenly upon the river up which he had ridden three times in his sleep.

There was no mistaking it. It was the very place. Yonder ran the swift brown waters, streaked with creamy foam. There hung the willow on the edge of the bank, with half of its roots exposed. And, above, the round hills tumbled away against the sky.

Macdonald covered his aching eyes with his

hands. The devil had brought him at last to the road of his death. He had no more doubt of that than though he had seen it written across the sky in letters of gold. He had no more doubt of it than though a voice had whispered it at his ear.

With a groan he surrendered to that feeling of fate. He turned Sunset up the stream and rode slowly on. In a sort of mute agony he watched the happy head of Sunset tossing, with his sharp ears quivering forward. Ah, to be a mere joyous brute like the big horse, to be freed from all these tortures of the mind that went with manhood.

He passed among the hills and came again to the ridge. With a sick heart he looked down upon that landscape which he had three times seen in his dream—the bright sun falling, the spotting shadows from the trees, and the far voices of the cattle. And who could struggle against such manifest destiny as this?

Riding down the slope, he twisted over the undulating surface of the plain, and so he came at last to the place where that avenue of walnut trees should have been. But here he found, for the first time, a difference between the dream and the reality. For the trees were gone, nor was there any semblance of them standing on either side of the road, but only a few wretched shrubs here and there. He had passed down the road for a mile or more, when he saw a buggy approaching with an old man driving it. He hailed the driver and stopped him.

"Friend," Macdonald said, "I want to ask you a few questions about this country. Have you been living around here long?"

"Not more'n about fifty years," said the old man, laughing with some importance.

"And you've known this road all that time?"

"Yep."

"Do you mind telling me if there were ever walnut trees growing along the sides of it?"

The other started. "How did you know that if you're a stranger in this here country, the way you say?"

But Macdonald rode to the side of the buggy and, leaning over, laid his hand on the shoulder of the other. "In the name of God," he said solemnly, "tell me the truth. There *have* been walnut trees planted here?"

"There have!" gasped the other, overwhelmed by the question and the manner in which it was put to him.

"Then God have mercy on my soul," groaned Macdonald, and spurred furiously down the road.

It was not long after this that he came upon the town itself, but he had hardly entered it before he began to recognize it, not as the thing he had seen in his dream—there was no silence here—but as a place where he had been before. Suddenly rounding a corner he came upon a blighting

299

proof. For this was the town that he had left two days before. Fortune had led him in a circle. He had come back by a new approach, and yonder, straight before him, was the very hotel itself, big and towered like a castle. He looked closer at it, with all the freshness of the dream weighing upon him. Yes, this was the castle of his vision. It was only the town house of the Moore family.

He stretched out his arms and laughed in the sunshine. A thousand tons of dread seemed to have been removed from his mind. There were still other things to be explained. He must find where he had seen that row of walnut trees other than in the dream. He must find where he had seen the girl.

At least he was now startled out of that absent-mindedness which, as a rule, plagued him and closed his eyes to things that were most familiar around him. He would see whatever was to be seen. As for Rory Moore, let him take heed to himself, or one portion of that dream would at least come true.

He went again to the hotel, again he asked for a room, and again he was assigned to the same chamber. There needed no explanation of the frightened eyes that men turned upon him, as he crossed the lobby and went up the stairs. They knew he had come back to kill Rory Moore. Well, their knowledge was doubly right.

Once in that room where the dream had twice

come to him, he looked sharply around him, and it was as though the scales had fallen from his eyes. He could see it all at a glance. Mystery? There was none at all. What he had half seen and left unnoted by his conscious mind, he was now keenly aware of, and here was all the substance of his dream.

Someone with no common touch had made those fading paintings that hung along the walls. There, a small sketch, was the narrow and rushing river streaking down from the ragged hills that rolled back against the sky. And here, too, was the sweeping bird's-eye view of the sunlit plain. But where was the girl?

He had only to turn to the opposite wall to see her, just as she had ridden into his dream, sitting lightly on the sidesaddle and riding around a curve down a long avenue of mighty walnut trees.

Here, then, had his dream gone out. But, as the first rush of relief left him, he was struck with a sharp little pang of grief. He had banished that dream and all that was in it. He had found the most simple of explanations. But what of the girl? By the fashion of that coat and the puffed shoulders, she was dead these many years, or else she had grown into middle age, something of her youth had died from her. She was dead, indeed, and he could never find her as he had seen her.

The door opened on the chambermaid with clean linen over her arm.

"Look here," Macdonald said to the old woman. "Have you ever known the girl in this picture?"

"Miss Mary Moore?" said the other. "Sure I knew her. Mind you, the man that painted that picture was her lover, and she died in a fall from that very same horse three days after that picture was painted. I mind it as well as if it was yesterday. I was a servant in this house then, and I've been here ever since."

Macdonald dismissed her with a dollar bill and returned to his own gloomy thoughts. He had gone for two days in what he considered an exquisite torment. But now he began to wonder if the torment into which he was passing might not be worse after all. For there had lingered in his mind, all those hours, the hope that someday he would find her, just as she had been when she rode into his dream. And if all the terror of the dream were gone, all the beauty of it was gone, too.

There was a light rap at the door, and he bade the person enter. It was a dusty, barefoot boy, with a letter in his hand, and great frightened eyes fixed upon the face of Macdonald, as though the latter had been an evil spirit. He was gone the instant the big man took the envelope. Macdonald tore it open and found within it the shortest and the most eloquent of notes:

I am waiting for you, just in front of the blacksmith shop.

Rory Moore

Methodically he tore the letter to bits. It was an old habit of his. Next, still out of force of habit, he took out his Colt and examined it from muzzle to the butt, polished by the years of use. Last of all he turned to the picture of Mary Moore. What he had seen in the dream was true enough. She was very like Rory. She might have posed as his sister.

XII

Like all events which grow in importance after they happen, and which become a part of even minor history, what happened that day was remembered even to the most minute details. And everyone of mature years in the town was able to recall some part. At least they had seen Macdonald issue from the hotel, dressed with unusual care, a flaming red bandanna around his throat, with the point hanging far down between his shoulders, and a great sombrero decorated with silver medallions upon his head, and his boots shined until they were like twin mirrors. One might have thought that he was going to be the best man at a wedding, or the groom himself.

But everyone knew that he was going out to give battle and take a life or give his own. For the rumor had passed, as swiftly as rumors do, through the length and the breadth of the town that Rory Moore was waiting in front of the blacksmith shop, and that he had sent a message to the terrible Macdonald.

So scores of eyes were watching as the big man walked down the single street of the village. He had never seemed taller. He had never seemed more sedate. He carried with him that unconscious air of importance that goes with men who have seen or suffered much.

He paused at the corner, where the corral from the hotel bordered the street. There he leaned against the fence and called. And the big red stallion came running to the voice of his new master. A dozen men swore that they saw Macdonald pass his arms around the neck of the horse and put his head down beside the head of Sunset.

Then he went on again with as light a stride as ever. When the watchers thought of Rory Moore, their hearts shrank within them. For it seemed impossible that such a force as Macdonald could be stopped by any one man.

More than one hardy cowpuncher set his teeth at the thought and looked to his gun. If anything happened to Rory, it would take all the desperate nerve and skill of a Macdonald to get out of that town. For they had determined that, fair play or not, the time had come to finish this destroyer of men.

In the meantime, Macdonald had passed the general merchandise store. He had come to the Perkins place, and there he paused to speak to an old Mexican beggar woman who came with a toothless whine to ask for money. They saw him take out a whole wad of rustling bills and drop it into her hand. The bills overflowed. She leaped upon them like an agile old beast of prey. When she straightened again, he was half a block away, and she poured out a shrill volley of blessings. Her borrowed English failed her, and to become truly eloquent she fell back upon the native Spanish and filled the air with it.

But her benefactor went on without a glance behind him.

"He's superstitious," said the beholders. "He's trying to get good luck for the meeting with Rory . . . and the devil take him and the old beggar."

But now he had come in sight of the blacksmith shop. A cluster of men fell back. One or two lingered beside Rory Moore, begging him to the last minute not to throw away his life in vain. But he tore himself away from them and strode well out into the street, where the fierce white sun beat down upon him. Nearer drew Macdonald, and still his bearing was as casual and light as the bearing of any pleasure seeker.

"Macdonald!" cried Rory Moore suddenly in a wild, hoarse voice.

"Well, Rory," answered the smooth tones of the man-killer, "are you ready?"

"Yes, curse you, ready!"

"Then get your gun!"

And Rory, waiting for no second invitation, reached for the butt of his Colt. It was an odd contrast that lay between the two, as they faced one another—Rory crouched over and taut with eagerness, and the tall and careless form of Macdonald. And it seemed that the same carelessness was in the gesture with which he reached for his weapon. Yet such was the consummate speed of that motion that his gun was bare before the revolver of Rory Moore was out of the holster. His gun was bare, but there seemed to be some slip. Carelessness had been carried too far, for the gun flashed in his hand and dropped into the dust.

And Rory? His own weapon exploded. It knocked up a little fountain of dust at the feet of the giant. He fired again and Macdonald collapsed backward like a falling tower. The big sombrero dropped from his head, and he lay with his long red hair floating like blood across the dust.

And yet so incredible was it to all who watched that Macdonald should indeed have fallen, that there was a long pause before a yell of triumph rose from a hundred throats, and they closed around the big man, like wolves around a dead lion.

And when the wonder of it was faded a little, they picked up his gun, where it had fallen in the dust. They picked it up, they examined it, as one might have examined the sword of Achilles, after the arrow had struck his heel, and the venom had worked. They broke the gun open. But not a bullet fell out. And then they saw that it was empty, and that Macdonald had come so carelessly down that street not to kill, but to be killed!

It was a thunderstroke to the townsmen. It was as though the devil, being trailed into a corner, should turn into an angel and take flight for heaven.

"There ain't more'n one way of looking at it," said the sheriff, when he came into the town that evening on a foaming horse. "Macdonald didn't want to kill young Moore. But he had to face him or be called a coward. And there you have it. He's been a hound all his life, but he's died like a hero."

And that was the motive behind the monument that was built for Macdonald in that town. Although partly, perhaps, they simply wanted to identify themselves with that terrible and romantic figure.

But, while the turmoil of talk was sweeping up

and down the town, two women were the first to think of striving to untangle the mysterious motives of Macdonald by something which he might have left behind him in his room—perhaps some letter to explain everything.

It was Mrs. Charles Moore who led the way, and with her went her niece, the sister of Rory. They found the room undisturbed, exactly as it had been when Macdonald left. But all they found was his rifle, his other revolver, his slicker, and his bedroll. There was nothing else except a few trifles. So they began to look around the room itself.

"And look yonder!" Mrs. Charles Moore cried. "There's the place he dumped out the bullets from his gun . . . poor man . . . right underneath the picture of your poor dead Aunt Mary. And, child, child, how astonishingly you've grown to be like her! I've never seen such a likeness . . . just in the last year you've sprouted up and grown into the very shadow of her."

"Oh," cried the girl, "how can you talk of such things."

"What in the world . . . ," began the other.

"Here in this very room . . . and . . . here where he thought his last thoughts."

"Heavens above, silly child, you're weeping for him!"

"But I saw him when they carried him in from the street," Mary said softly, with the tears running slowly down her face. "And even in death he seemed a greater man than any I'll ever see. And one great arm and hand was hanging down . . . I shall never forget."

ABOUT THE AUTHOR

Max Brand is the best-known pen name of Frederick Faust, creator of Dr. Kildare, Destry, and many other fictional characters popular with readers and viewers worldwide. Faust wrote for a variety of audiences in many genres. His enormous output, totaling approximately thirty million words or the equivalent of five hundred thirty ordinary books, covered nearly every field: crime, fantasy, historical romance, espionage, Westerns, science fiction, adventure, animal stories, love, war, and fashionable society, big business and big medicine. Eighty motion pictures have been based on his works along with many radio and television programs. For good measure, he also published four volumes of poetry. Perhaps no other author has reached more people in such a variety of different ways.

Born in Seattle in 1892, orphaned early, Faust grew up in the rural San Joaquin Valley of California. At Berkeley he became a student rebel and one-man literary movement, contributing prodigiously to all campus publications. Denied a degree because of unconventional conduct, he embarked on a series of adventures culminating in New York City where, after a period of near starvation, he received simultaneous recognition as a serious poet and successful author of fiction. Later, he traveled widely, making his home in New York, then in Florence, Italy, and finally in Los Angeles.

Once the United States entered the Second World War, Faust abandoned his lucrative writing career and his work as a screenwriter to serve as a war correspondent with the infantry in Italy, despite his fifty-one years and a bad heart. He was killed during a night attack on a hilltop village held by the German army. New books based on magazine serials or unpublished manuscripts or restored versions continue to appear so that, alive or dead, he has averaged a new book every six months for seventy-five years. Beyond this, some work by him is newly reprinted every week of every year in one or another format somewhere in the world. A great deal more about this author and his work can be found in *The Max Brand Companion* (Greenwood Press, 1997) edited by Jon Tuska and Vicki Piekarski. His Website is www.MaxBrandOnline.com.

Books are produced in the United States using U.S.-based materials

Books are printed using a revolutionary new process called THINKtech™ that lowers energy usage by 70% and increases overall quality

Books are durable and flexible because of Smyth-sewing

Paper is sourced using environmentally responsible foresting methods and the paper is acid-free

Center Point Large Print
600 Brooks Road / PO Box 1
Thorndike, ME 04986-0001 USA

(207) 568-3717

US & Canada:
1 800 929-9108
www.centerpointlargeprint.com